Dark Steps

Brian Hershey

Reader2writer Press
www.reader2writer.com

Paperback: 978-0-578-86607-9
eBook: 978-0-578-86608-6

Library of Congress Number: 2021936155

First paperback edition April 2021.

Edited by Kayla Hardin & Bart Bishop
Cover art by Brendon Miller

Printed by Reader2writer Press in the USA.

Reader2writer Press
Cincinnati, Ohio

www.reader2writer.com

To the English Department of Northern Kentucky University, thank you for encouraging me to write this story!

The ability to become aware of something through the senses is perception. For most, this is reality. Though often it is just a veil that covers sins that hide below the surface of the outward impression of normalcy, worsened by the gift of free will.

Prologue

"This can't be happening! Please stop!" Doreane Moore said as she scurried backward along the floor desperately trying to escape. The blow was fast to her forehead, knocking her momentarily senseless. "St-stop…please," she whimpered "Why–why are you doing this?"

The second blow came with an equal amount of force upon her mouth. She rolled to her stomach and spit her front teeth onto the hardwood floor. Blood poured over her lips as she attempted to drag herself into the next room.

With a sudden jerk, Doreane felt her body being yanked from behind. She was losing all sense of awareness. Her eyes were blurry, and she choked on her own blood. When her body came to a stop, she glanced to her left. The searing pain in her head made it hard to focus on the body of her husband, Jamal. He was unconscious, lying on his back. His nose appeared as though it had been crushed inward.

"No, no–no, baby no!" she whimpered as her husband's body was rolled on its stomach. The first strike to the back of his head came with the wicked sound of his skull cracking. The second strike splattered his blood across the side of her face, forcing her to close her eyes. Each heavy, forceful blow crushed more of her husband's skull until the strikes sounded wet and mawkish. The final blow broke the boards of the hardwood floor.

A weighty constraint prevented Doreane from moving. A hand gripped her hair. It was extremely strong, and she didn't have the strength to fight it. The hits to her head and face were too much. Dizziness mixed with pain.

"Lucas," Doreane uttered just before she heard the same wicked crack of her own skull, and everything in the room went dark.

1

Not dead, though certainly devoid of any enthusiasm for life, Derrick Mayes listened to the snow pelt the windowpane of his apartment as an empty shiver ran the length of his body. Too much bourbon from the night before had caused a headache to split his temples with the slightest movement. The digital clock on his nightstand glowed bright against the darkened room and read 6:44 a.m., one minute before it would shriek its tones to announce the end of the night's slumber; piercing, painful, breaking the quietness of the room.

Working for Jobs and Family Services in Cincinnati produced nothing more than a constant feeling of exhaustion after sixty to seventy-hour work weeks that hid behind the guise of operating for the "greater good." No satisfaction, no enjoyment, Derrick's work was merely a collection of moments strung together into hours and days, lost within the folds of endless paperwork and bad memories that couldn't be erased. He had come to refer to his clientele as the *invisible society*. They often contributed nothing, never left their homes, never participated in community events or activities, and never supported institutions such as libraries or schools. Yet, they were happy to take from the community and were often perpetrators of horrific abuse to their children. Exhausting. Draining. *Leeches*, Derrick thought as he forced himself to sit up in his bed and hit the button on the clock to avoid the alarm. Even after twenty-two years of experience as both a case worker and a therapist, most of his clients worked against him. He was *not* someone they wanted to come to their homes. JFS had the stigma of being child snatchers, homewreckers, and a general menace to a community in the eyes of the ignorant.

Derrick's head throbbed. A fifth of Maker's Mark stood beside a small picture of his late wife, Hannah. He grasped the framed photo and let it come to rest on his lap as he rubbed the nape of his neck with his other hand. In an attempt to blink away the haziness of sleep and stabilize the pulses of discomfort in his head, Derrick focused on the warm image. It captured a moment that was happy, but gone. Car accident, so fast, no warning, just gone. Hollowness was all he felt; a longing to have her back in his life, to feel her touch, her breath against his rough skin, intimacy, another chance at having a family. The red glow from the digital clock shown through the bottle of whiskey and cast a reddish-brown hue onto the picture making it appear more sinister, almost symbolic of her death.

Two years had passed since the tragic accident, yet Derrick's pain remained. Most attempts at offering support from family and friends exasperated the void inside. One by one people had returned to their own sense of normalcy, but Hannah was dead and nothing comforting could be said to change that, and very little alleviated the pain. Alcohol merely numbed it, but that was the best he could do.

A twinge of sadness formed in Derrick's stomach. He didn't have the mindset to delve into the joyful memory of Hannah playfully turning away from the camera with rays of sunlight kissing her chestnut-colored cheeks as the tight curls of her hair dangled across her forehead. She was loving, kind, simply beautiful. Haphazardly, he tossed the picture onto the bed. In need of a distraction, Derrick reached for his cell phone, but paused to glance at his laptop. *Later, not now… you can't watch…not now*, he thought. Pressing the home button on his phone revealed three missed calls from the night before. Bourbon was the reason he missed them. *Too much of that stuff too.* He swiped the screen to listen.

Message one received Tuesday, January eighth at seven forty p.m. Mr. Mayes…this is Mary Ellen Ferguson, and this is the third time I have called you about Jeremiah. I have filed all the necessary paperwork with the agency, and I was approved to be the foster parent, so I don't know what the hold-up is. Since you're his legal guardian, could you call me back at…

He deleted the message before it was through. Demanding, annoying, and generally unpleasant, Mary Ellen was a person that could find the raw nerve of emotion in Derrick. He knew her number and was purposely avoiding her. Mary Ellen had been a foster parent through the agency before and this gave her a sense of entitlement. She felt that the agency should personally thank her for her service to the community or at least treat her with higher regard than the others seeking to foster children. Mary Ellen was not shy about telling people this either. It was widely rumored that she, like most of the foster parents in the system Derrick knew, was only doing it for the government stipend rather than a genuine care for the children. Despite her greed, the home was at least clean and accommodating. Derrick had hoped that a family would adopt Jeremiah, a nine-year-old client of his, before she had a chance to work the system any further.

Message two received Tuesday, January eighth at eight-fifteen p.m. Derrick, Honey…it's your mother. I was hoping that you would be able to give me a ride to church tomorrow evening…Cough, Cough! Don't feel like you have to, if not I'll just take the bus again.

Her voice was raspy, weak and the cold usually brought on labored breathing. She was also prone to infection. Every Wednesday, Derrick's mother would attend church service, for fellowship, prayer, and an evening meal followed by bible study. *She can't ride the bus,* Derrick thought. *In Avondale, at night, in the cold–I don't think so. Some asshole is dying to take advantage of that.* His mother knew Derrick's anxiety over the situation and would leave him the same message each Tuesday, mostly as an attempt to get him to return to church.

Derrick hadn't been back to the church since before Hannah died. Church often made him feel worse about his situation. Too many well-wishers tried to make him feel good about a dire situation, instead of letting the natural grieving process unfold. Senior Pastor Marcus was one of the worst offenders of such things, often denouncing the feelings inside of Derrick by claiming that the pain was still present because his heart wasn't aligned with God. Flashy, loud, even during prayer vigils, Pastor Marcus would go on tangents during his sermons that often ended in hell and damnation, a topic that Derrick explicitly wanted to avoid. Even a simple conversation with the man usually led to the same end. Worse, Mary Ellen Ferguson attended the same church and Derrick knew that she would certainly try to corner him about Jeremiah.

Like always, I'll just tell mom that I have too much to do in order to stay, he thought. *I'll just take my Chromebook, find an empty parking lot somewhere and review my e-mails while I wait for her to be done.* Derrick deleted the second message.

Head throbbing and dizzy, he stumbled to the bathroom. Little things were a struggle. It took several taps on the screen of his phone to play the third message on speaker. He laid it on the edge of the sink counter and turned on the water for a shower. The message started the same as the others.

Message three received Tuesday, January eighth at eleven fifty p.m. Derrick…it's Debra from Children's. I'm sorry to bother you so late. I wouldn't have called if it wasn't important. I already placed a call into in-take at JFS requesting you as the caseworker, but I wanted to speak with you personally about the case before in-take does. I know you're extremely busy, but please call me back as soon as you get this. I tru-ly need your help.

Dr. Debra Evans was one of the child psychiatrists for Children's Hospital. She had been friends with Derrick for years. They had collaborated on countless cases, including ones where Derrick was the assigned therapist. Though Derrick had stopped seeing clients as a therapist, Dr. Evens often requested him as the caseworker when there were heavier situations. Ones that involved serious abuse. The nasty, violent type, or the cases where children were viciously assaulted, sexually. Derrick sat broodingly on the edge of the toilet as the dread seeped into his consciousness. Slowly, he shook his head. "No," he whispered. "She'll have to find someone else."

Thoughts of older cases poured into his already crowded brain. Three years prior, a non-accidental head injury of an eleven-year-old, Jared, in January 2012, the mother was convicted of child cruelty and sentenced to 18 months imprisonment. The child never recovered fully, only to divulge in his suicide note written the day of his mother's release from prison that the abuse had been ongoing, not an isolated incident. Little over one year prior, the death of an eight-year-old, Layla, in November 2014 was the result of asphyxia caused by *ligature strangulation*. Father apparently got carried away during what he had called a discipline session, but was sentenced to two life terms after the autopsy report had revealed his semen in the young girl's vaginal canal. It was a case that was initially disguised as intense social anxiety, possible Glossophobia, in which Derrick was simply trying to get the girl to talk. Shaking his head in disgust he murmured, "I can't–I can't. Fifty-two kids–too many to manage as it is. Debra knows this. I can't do it."

Derrick removed his clothes and stepped into the shower. The hot water ran over the back of his neck and shoulders as he let his head hang. There was something in Debra's voice that was haunting. It clung to the last line of the message before it trailed off. *I tru-ly need your help.* Intermixed with the dread of the case, this line quickly embedded itself deep into the realization that he didn't really have a choice in the matter. JFS wasn't going to let him get out of a case where a doctor personally requested him as the caseworker. Derrick knew how this would unfold. *Coming from Children's–agency is probably gonna close out a different case where there are less severe allegations; that doesn't require weekly or biweekly visits, to make room for this new case,* Derrick thought. He finished his shower. Water swirled for a moment before draining. Drops fell; an empty hollow silence followed. *Damn!*

He made his way back to his bedroom. The hardwood floor of his apartment was chilly, and the snow continued to pelt the windows. This only added to Derrick's distress. Driving in this weather, this snowy mess made everything worse. He still had to report to his assigned kids regardless of how bad it was outside. Derrick could only hope for a state-of-emergency situation to get out of seeing his clients, though it would make for a busy, difficult weekend to make up the utilization hours the agency needed to produce to stay operative under state requirements.

Shea butter lotion was the only thing that kept his dark skin from being ashy during the winter months. Everywhere he went the dry heat was cranked up or required the use of a spray bottle with 91% rubbing alcohol in it. This killed the bedbug eggs and anything else that wanted to hitch a ride. The lotion also covered the liquor smell that would sometimes emanate from his pores when he got overheated after a night of drinking. Most importantly, Hannah always used it. Rubbing the thick lotion over his arms and legs brought back a brief, but sweet memory of her.

The more he moved the better his hangover headache got. It wasn't long before Derrick was dressed and ready to leave. He took a big drink of water and swallowed two ibuprofen to take care of the remaining hangover traces. No breakfast, but at least he wasn't going to have to fight a muddled reality enhanced by a nauseating headache.

Outside the daylight had broken into the sky, but the dark gray clouds remained, threatening to snow more at any moment. Wind gusted bits of snow and ice. Only a few inches of accumulation, and for the most part the roads were dry. It was cold, too cold to be outside for long. Exposed skin in single-digit weather did damage, fast. Derrick adjusted his beanie cap and made sure his Peacoat was fully buttoned. The wool Peacoat wasn't enough to fend against the wintery air, but it was enough to walk from the parking lots to the buildings. He sat inside his 2009 Grand Cherokee as it warmed up. The carport kept most of the snow off but did nothing for the frigid temperature.

Lower Price Hill…west of downtown…first scheduled stop of the day, Derrick thought. *Debra's at Children's just off I-71 South…easy stop. Maybe I can convince her to take another caseworker or something.* Derrick pulled out of the parking lot with a strong, inauspicious sensation that swirled in the pit of his stomach.

He had no idea what to expect when he pulled into Children's. The walkways were shoveled and drier looking, but the wind cut into him mercilessly. Derrick walked through the automated doors and was immediately met with an uncomfortable feeling as though the eyes of everyone were upon him. Accusing him, judging him. His hair spiked on the back of his neck. His stomach churned with a light queasiness that scraped through his veins like ice fragments. Trying not to draw too much attention to himself, Derrick moved to one of the cushioned chairs in the foyer to steady himself from a strange dizzy sensation. "Too–too much to drink," he whispered as he rubbed his temples, hoping that no hospital workers he knew would recognize him in this obviously still drunken state.

A few moments passed as his composure returned and the ill feeling receded a little. Derrick took several deep breaths before making his way to the water fountain to take more than a few gulps. Dorothy Chase was working the information desk. He knew her well and greeted her with the same cheerful smile that he always did when making an unannounced visit to the hospital, yet his croaky voice couldn't hide his current state. "Good morning Dorothy."

"Good morning Derrick. Cold one out there today," she replied with delight. She was in her sixties, always smiling. Derrick was envious of her life. Despite having worked for Children's for the past thirty-two years in the same position, she was happy. Pictures of her children and grandchildren surrounded her workspace. It looked inviting and cozy. "I don't think it's going to be much better for the rest of the week into next. Single digits I heard."

Fortunately, Dorothy wasn't attuned to Derrick's ill feelings and certainly didn't treat him with any variance than normal. "God, I hope not. I'm not sure I'll be able to handle it for much longer."

"Well, this is Ohio, and you know that winter sort of drags on around here. Anyway, enough of the pleasantries, I know you didn't come here for small talk with an old biddy like me. Watcha need hun?"

"Debra left me a message last night about a new intake. I was hoping to catch her before I went to the rest of my appointments."

"Hang on dear, lemme see if she's in." Dorothy glanced back to her computer and began clicking the mouse. Derrick placed his cell phone and keys on the front counter, removed his gloves, and leaned one elbow on the surface. He hoped that the strange feeling he had when he arrived wasn't going to endure. The last thing that he needed was to be sick in front of Dorothy, Debra, or anyone else for that matter. Dorothy looked back at him. "Looks like she's here. Fourth floor, she was on-call last night, came in late, and has been here ever since."

"Thanks Dorothy. You're a gem. I'm going to head up and see if I can catch her." Derrick felt his stomach churning again as he started to walk away from Dorothy when she called out to him.

"Derrick!" He faced her again, a clear, anxious look on his face. "Forgetting something?"

Derrick looked to where Dorothy was pointing and saw his keys and cell phone still resting atop the counter. "Right! Thank you. Can't forget these."

"Are you feeling okay Derrick?"

"Yeah–I'm fine. It's just the cold. Scratchy throat– makes me tired." Derrick grabbed his cell phone and keys.

Dorothy half smiled but watched him prudently as he made his way toward the elevator. Once inside, he unbuttoned his coat and leaned against the rail along the wall of the elevator. *She knows. She's no fool*, he thought. *Dorothy knows you drink.*

Derrick took several deep breaths to stave off the ill feeling in his stomach. *Possibly the ibuprofen. But at least my headache has dissolved.* The doors to the elevator dinged, then opened into a small foyer and a nurses' station with multi-colored hallways that extended down the right and left side.

Derrick stepped out and immediately began scanning the area for Dr. Evans. He approached the nurses' station. "Excuse–" Just as he was about to inquire about Dr. Evans's whereabouts, Derrick heard a familiar voice.

"Ahh. I'm glad you got my message." Dr. Evans rounded the corner with a large cup of coffee in her hands. She was wearing her lab coat over a thick sweater, her hair pulled back into a short ponytail. Derrick always found her to be attractive and often thought of *'what if'* with Dr. Evans before he married Hannah. Dark circles were only partially concealed by her squared-framed glasses. Though attractive, she looked tired.

Derrick leaned to one side, raised his eyebrows, and expressed dismay for her worn-out appearance. Yet, it was more so for the ill feelings he had toward accepting another case on top of his already overwhelming caseload. "I got your message this morning. Debra–"

"Before you throw out your objections, let's talk."

Dr. Evans ushered Derrick past the nurses' station to a waiting area with conjoining olive-green chairs that formed a partial square around a white round table that had a few magazines strewn across it. They sat next to each other as Dr. Evans placed her coffee cup on one of the smaller corner tables between the armless green chairs. "Derrick, I need your help."

"I know. You mentioned that in the message," Derrick responded with a slight level of irritation.

Dr. Evans pursed her lips, cluing into Derrick's touchiness. "Look, intake's going to give you this case whether you want it or not. Let me just state that for the record. But, we do have a very serious situation Derrick. Alex and I got a nasty one last night--"

"Leverty?" Derrick interrupted. Dr. Evens nodded yes. "Physically or sexually abused?" Derrick asked.

"Neither, as far as we can tell."

"Then why did you call me? You and Dr. Leverty can handle this. I mean come on, you know I have a heavy caseload," Derrick spat. He rubbed his temples.

"The police are involved in this one."

"The police are always involved, Debra! Why do you need me?" Derrick's voice was louder, but he stopped as Dr. Evans held up her hand to quiet him down. He reached for his stomach after his outburst and proceeded to rub his temples again.

Dr. Evans sighed. "Jesus, Derrick, you haven't been drinking again, have you?" Derrick simply offered a scornful look with the tilt of his head. Dr. Evans sighed again. "Sorry. I know–off-topic–and none of my business. Derrick, the child that came in last night witnessed his parents' murder!"

Derrick leaned back against the chair he was sitting on and let his arms come to rest on either side of his legs. "So–what do want me to do? You know I don't see clients anymore as a therapist, if that's what you're implying." His voice was softer, more forgiving than before. Yet, he was very attuned to what she was asking. "Why did you mention the police?"

"It's because of the nature of the crime."

"Murder is murder."

"Not like this." Derrick leaned forward slowly and focused more on Dr. Evans. "Both parents had their heads crushed in from the back beyond the point of any recognition."

"Wait–heads were crushed in from the back? How would that affect facial recognition?"

"The killer repeatedly struck the back of their heads until nearly nothing remained atop their necks. Their faces were crushed into the floor of their apartment."

Derrick felt his face contort in disgust. "The child- was he or she injured, harmed, anything?"

"*He*, and outside of some malnourishment, no. First responders found him hunched inside a nearby closet under some coats after a neighbor had called about the smell. Initial reports state that they were killed three days ago...and it appears that young Lucas Moore hadn't moved from his hiding spot since. Not even so much as a drop of blood on him, but he's catatonic and hasn't spoken to us yet. Poor child probably saw the whole thing happen." Dr. Evans uncrossed her legs and looked down at the floor. "Probably Acute Stress Disorder, PTSD, it's hard to say what may be causing his current state. Lord knows, he's going to have a slew of problems as he gets older."

"Debra. You still haven't told me why you need me," Derrick said as he leaned his elbows on his knees and crossed his fingertips.

"The detectives are pushing hard to catch the person responsible and considering that Lucas is the only eyewitness-" Dr. Evans held up her hands as if to suggest there was nothing else she could say.

"Again, you don't really need *me*."

"He might respond to a male therapist better than me, a black male therapist."

"He's African American?" Derrick clarified.

"Yes. Plus, until this goes through the courts, JFS has custody. With the police leaning hard on us to get him to talk, I don't want anyone else on this case except those who I know will give him the best care and can help me explain the situation to them."

Derrick took in a deep breath and released it in a long, controlled exhale. His voice was low, hoarse, "Alright…alright, I'll help any way I can."

2

Wintry bursts of wind had stopped by mid-day but had left the outside temperature in the teens, which fell close to single digits as the sun set. Though Derrick's apartment was cold, it was warmer than sitting in his car checking his email, and waiting for his mother to finish her church service. But she was home safe, not waiting in the frigid air. Derrick was free to do things that he wanted but was frustrated that he still had work items that needed to be completed. As usual, helping his mother cost him time. The furnace kicked on as he entered his apartment and hadn't shut off since. It was cold, secluded from the rest of the world.

The gooseneck lamp on Derrick's desk illuminated his workspace enough that he could type on his Chromebook, but it wasn't enough to light the entire room. Derrick sat in his chair and rotated his neck from side-to-side. It cracked once and he held it to one side, stretching the muscles to alleviate the tension headache he had acquired throughout the day. A sigh into a heavy breath escaped past his lips. *Why did Debra have to give me this case*, he thought before entering the daily log.

Log: January 9th, 2019

I met with one new file today that has come through the screeners and followed up with three other older cases: Case ONE: **New**–African American male, 10 years of age, found in a catatonic state after witnessing the murder of his parents three days ago. No siblings and no family members have been located. Malnourished, yet otherwise unscathed. Initial diagnosis: Catatonia brought about by Posttraumatic Stress Disorder. R/O: Generalized Anxiety Disorder (Acute) and Adjustment Disorder. Source: Cincinnati Police Department, Referral from Children's Hospital, Debra Evans, MD was the attending physician…

Derrick stopped typing and sipped his newly poured glass of bourbon. The Maker's Mark burned his throat before rolling over into the smoky maltiness characteristic of the bourbon. Derrick closed his eyes and exhaled deeply. The alcohol vapors passed through his nostrils.

His personal laptop computer was charging on the corner of his desk. A twinge of excitement manifested in his loins at the thought of indulging in porn. His chest tightened with anticipation. To Derrick, it was likened to that of heroin, a temptation, an addiction that was a temporary fix, a rush of exhilaration that often led to worsened feelings of emptiness. He knew it. He felt it. It was the only thing that filled the biological need of sex, but it was never as fulfilling as the intimacy that he and Hannah shared. Nonetheless, it was what replaced the physical act of making love that he had rationalized as a safe means of a sexual experience. Something that also kept at bay the darker, more sinister loneliness that had often crept in during the bitter, dismal hours. *Finish your work first then you're free to watch*, Derrick thought.

…Heavy police involvement with this case and there is the expectation of therapeutic services along with case file management. No court date has been established for fostering. JFS has gained temporary custody and will help facilitate court proceedings and placement within foster care or residency home upon release from the hospital. I decided that I would provide additional therapeutic services in an attempt at helping the child to regain his sense of awareness.

My initial observation of him was as Dr. Evans had reported. He was catatonic, staring blankly at the floor in front of him. The boy showed no conscious signs of response to verbal prompts or even physical stimuli by Dr. Evans. A follow-up visit has been scheduled for Friday afternoon to allow the hospital personnel to treat the malnourishment while monitoring his adjustment progress to his new surroundings.

Lucas Moore…poor bastard's not going to have a fair chance at life, Derrick thought. *PTSD, anxiety, adjustment disorder…hmmm…they'll be with him for the rest of his life, if he even comes out of it. Just another fucking statistic in the system*. Derrick shot down the remainder of his bourbon. He leaned back in his chair and placed his hands behind his head. The bourbon warmed his belly and helped to fend off the chill that was ever present inside his apartment. He took several long, deep breaths, allowing the euphoric buzz of the bourbon to ease his mind. The nausea he felt at the hospital had fully subsided. It was strange how fast it came on. Driving along the freeway, Derrick had felt fine, uneasy, but otherwise normal. *Don't drink so much tonight. No more fucking ibuprofen on an empty stomach either.*

> Case TWO–Allegations of a dirty house, unsanitary for children. Upon arrival, feces, roaches, minimal amounts of proper food, house smelled really bad. There are three alleged child victims in the residence ages 4, 7, and 11. Mother recovering heroin addict, has been given three days to make significant changes to the home environment before the agency assumes custody of the children present. Mother was given numbers to the local food bank and shelters should the home environment require more in-depth improvements.

The bottle of bourbon was in the kitchen. *Another glass won't hurt me.* Derrick had drunk himself to sleep the night before. It was one of those nights where the thought of ending all the pain would be swift with a quick squeeze of his .38 Special's trigger. No more routine, no more shit, no more feelings of emptiness and loss. No more missing Hannah. Over, just like that. Derrick filled the glass halfway with bourbon. No ice, straight. His gun was in the drawer below the counter, fully loaded. *No…no. You still have someone who counts on you. Mom will be all alone.*

The voice in his head was a rational one, calculated and analytical. But, Derrick was running out of rational explanations. He had grown to hate his life, the burden and the negative crap that filled his entire world, relentless like the waves that crash upon the seashore, over and over again. Nothing he did seemed to make a difference. Placing children in foster care carried no sense of elation, no satisfaction. Holding parents accountable for the things they did to their children or were neglecting to do for their children only produced enemies and sapped his energy. No meaningful working relationships, or any meaningful relationships for that matter, no signs of appreciation for the number of hours that were dedicated to the job, to helping, to servicing those in need. Everywhere he turned, someone else was trying to take something from him: his pastor, Mary Ellen Ferguson. Derrick had even come to view his mother in such a way, but most of all it was his job. There was never enough time to complete the duties required of a caseworker or a therapist. Never time to enjoy the earnings, to enjoy a new car, a house, a fancy meal. Derrick's life had become routine, a bad one.

"I need a distraction," he whispered. Bringing the glass of bourbon to his lips, Derrick bottomed-up and swallowed the newly poured alcohol in two gulps. Returning to his work area, he clicked the save icon for his log and temporarily closed his Chromebook. Derrick never viewed anything unbecoming or even non-work related on his Chromebook. There was too much risk of being caught by the tech guys that policed the inappropriate use of the computers. Instead, he grabbed his fully charged laptop from the corner of his desk, opened it, and clicked on the search engine icon to begin, to start his distraction but continue his addiction. Derrick soon found himself in a euphoric, arousal bliss, partly from the alcohol, mostly from the porn.

3

Thursday blew past in a blur of frosty weather and hellish follow-ups to homes that Derrick had no desire to visit. Most were in Delhi, and one was in Lower Price Hill. Poverty, but mainly drug abuse, within the homes had brought about decay. Once a person had given into the destructive tendencies of heroin or other addictive substances, the effects were fast and obvious. It would start with garbage and mold, then bugs, bugs of all kinds. Bedbugs were awful to contend with, expensive, and difficult to get rid of if they managed to hitch a ride on something like a courier bag or even in the cuff of a pant leg. Yet, cockroaches were worse for Derrick. Each of the homes he went into had infestations of both, and the roaches always made him shiver a bit more. Roaches climbed the walls and scurried behind cabinetry and picture frames to find cozy places to lay eggs. Foul, mold-encrusted food littered the countertops and covered the unwashed dishes that had been neglected for seemingly several days. This drew in the cockroaches. Despite the number of years he had been a part of the agency, Derrick never fully got used to the horrific conditions that he witnessed in the homes he visited or investigated.

Occasionally, though, he did get a reprieve. Cases like Lucas's where the child had been hospitalized or institutionalized at least allowed for a clean environment, offered a brief break from the disgusting conditions that he was forced to visit. Children's was a great place. Besides the highly sanitized conditions, Derrick also found that there was less of the bureaucratic bullshit and stipulations required to treat children. They truly focused entirely on servicing the medical needs of children, both physically and mentally. Getting a child admitted to Children's was an oasis in a desert of bug-infested excrement.

Derrick stood outside of Lucas's room and reviewed the diagnosis from the Diagnostic Assessment Form. His stomach churned with nausea. *Slow down the drinking. Someone is going to notice,* he thought.

☒ AXIS I: 308.3 Acute Stress Disorder

☐ AXIS I: 309.81Posttraumatic Stress Disorder

☐ AXIS II: 309.24 Adjustment Disorder w/Anxiety

☐ AXIS III: Malnutrition, Medical history unknown

☐ AXIS IV: Unknown

☐ AXIS V: N/A GAF: Previous GAF: N/A

Comments: 308.3 Acute Stress Disorder, 309.81Posttraumatic Stress Disorder, 309.24 Adjustment Disorder w/Anxiety. No change in Catatonia.

Dr. Evans had kept the diagnosis the same, except now she wasn't trying to *rule out* an adjustment disorder. Instead, it was part of Lucas's secondary diagnosis. Acute Stress Disorder was the main focus. Nothing else really could be focused on until the symptoms of that were alleviated.

"He hasn't changed." Derrick looked up from the document at Dr. Evans who was walking toward him. "The only thing we've been able to really do is get him hydrated again and provide nutrients intravenously."

"Is that the reason for the adjustment disorder diagnosis?" Derrick asked as he rubbed his stomach to help quell the volatile feeling.

Dr. Evans just nodded as she pursed her lips at Derrick's obvious discomfort. He knew he had a problem; a fact Derrick was sure Dr. Evans was also well aware of. Fortunately for him, she kept the conversation on Lucas this time. "We figured that being in a different environment–a better environment along with some much-needed rest and nutrition that he might come to again. Unfortunately, this is what we have. Physically, he's healthy. No injuries, nutrition is better, all the tests we ran are normal, no abnormalities whatsoever. If he stays like this, we'll have to admit him to a residency facility so he can receive intense psychotherapy."

Dr. Evans looked at Derrick, but he merely nodded in return. Beds were at a premium at Children's Hospital and if the child was deemed physically sound, but still had mental health issues that didn't involve self-harm or harm to others, the child was often transferred to a facility that focused on rehabilitation with therapists. "Have you been able to locate any family members?" Derrick asked, dodging the implication that Dr. Evans was suggesting.

"An uncle from out of state, but we haven't been able to speak directly to him. Only voice messages." She paused before continuing. "Derrick, I'm not going to be able to keep a bed for him. JFS is going to need to get him into a residency program for treatment."

"Look, you know that going to a residency facility isn't as easy as simply saying it. There's more bullshit. Being here is probably the best for him at the moment. And with the police–"

"Excuse me, Dr. Evans?" a robust female voice cut in from a little way down the hallway. The woman was wearing a navy-colored overcoat that was still buttoned to the brim as though she had just come in from the cold. It hung to just past her knees revealing a dark pair of slacks that ran over a pair of winter, but stylish boots. Her hair, a weave, judging by the perfect lay of the large curls despite the intense winds that had picked up again outside, looked unscathed. Poised with confidence and an intelligent aura, the woman approached both Dr. Evans and Derrick. "Dr. Evans, I'm fortunate that I was able to catch up with you. I was wondering if you have a moment to discuss the case?"

Dr. Evans turned back to Derrick. "Derrick, this is Detective–"

"Mitchell. Detective Mitchell from the Cincinnati Police Department." She extended her hand and Derrick shook it. There was strength in her grip and keenness in her eyes that suggested she was studying Derrick, almost sizing him up with just a simple shake of the hand.

"Derrick–Mayes, JFS."

"Derrick is the caseworker that will be handling Lucas's placements and transitions in the upcoming days," Dr. Evans added.

"Well, it's a pleasure to meet you sir. If I may–" Detective Mitchell released Derrick's hand so that she could undo a button on her coat to retrieve a business card from within the inside pocket. "Here, I also heard that you'll be conducting some therapeutic services with Lucas as well and I would certainly like to be informed of any improvements in Lucas's condition."

Derrick took the card from the detective and slid it into the courier bag he had slung over his right shoulder, his stomach growing more upset by the second. Perhaps it was still the alcohol or maybe the fact that Detective Mitchell was so overbearing that made him nervous, uneasy. "Well, my client's condition is protected by HIPPA and seeing that JFS has custody and temporary guardianship–"

"Detective Mitchell, I'll be happy to speak with you now," Dr. Evans interjected before Derrick could finish. A curious look spread across the face of Detective Mitchell, but she remained poised and unabashed by her own request, despite Derrick's HIPPA comment. Her eyes studied him for a moment more before turning back to Dr. Evans with a polite smile. "The hospital has already agreed to fully cooperate in the investigation. Derrick was unaware of this and is merely doing what he is trained to do," Dr. Evans said to keep up professional relationships, but gave Derrick a sideways glance. It was clear that the detective wasn't used to being challenged. Her body language suggested to Derrick that the seriousness of the case was greater than what he had originally anticipated.

"Very well. Thank you, Dr. Evans. Mr. Mayes, it was a pleasure meeting you and we'll be in touch."

"Derrick, I assume you're going to meet with Lucas now?" Derrick nodded still eyeing the detective cautiously. Too many times in his career had he seen others provide information about cases too quickly to individuals without proper documentation, which usually resulted in their dismissal from the agency. "You know how to call the nurses' station and Dr. Leverty is on the floor doing his rounds if you need him and will be here for the rest of the night. I'll text you later."

Derrick had dealt with many police officers in the past. Generally, they were easy to work with and had a level of relatability to his work that most of the public did not. Yet, occasionally there were cases, like Lucas's, where police involvement was heavier than normal, and they weren't as sensitive to the privacy laws due to the horrific nature of the situations. It was understandable though. Brutal, graphic murders were upsetting to an entire community.

Derrick watched Detective Mitchell and Dr. Evans disappear around the corner before he opened the door and entered Lucas's room. Derrick paused at the door for a second to take a few deep breaths. The feeling of being sick was stronger. Inside, the room was like any other hospital room, except more colorful. Lucas was sitting on the edge of the hospital bed, dressed in nothing but a gown and grippy socks provided to all patients. He was staring directly out the window along the far wall as if hypnotized by something extraordinary. There was nothing but an overcast sky. Derrick belched quietly, before moving toward Lucas. A stabbing pain formed in his stomach.

"Good morning, Lucas," Derrick stated in a soft but assertive tone as he sat in one of the cushioned chairs within the room. He wanted to sound as friendly and as non-threatening as he could, given the state of his stomach. "My name is Mr. Mayes. I'm a friend of Dr. Evans, the nice lady that has been trying to help you." There was no response from Lucas. He didn't even acknowledge that Derrick was even in the room. Instead, he remained frozen in his catatonic state, mouth slightly agape, staring at seemingly nothing. "Lucas, I was hoping that we might be able to talk about how you got here. Would you be okay with that?" Still, nothing.

Derrick sighed. He placed his courier bag on the floor next to the chair as he stood up and moved toward Lucas's bedside. Standing a couple of feet away from Lucas, Derrick moved his hand in a slow, sweeping motion to disrupt the sight pattern of Lucas. He wanted to see if Lucas would flinch or even if there was any involuntary eye movement. Nothing. Not so much as a blink of the eyelids. The child remained completely still, motionless, bereft to even involuntary movements of the eyes. Derrick placed his hands on his hips and sighed, knowing full well that it was not going to be easy to get

Lucas to open up and talk. *Think, think. What does Lucas need?* This thought was repetitive, but an answer was unattainable now. The churning discomfort in his stomach was becoming a horrendous distraction.

The door creaked open. Corey Coleman, a male nurse that was assigned to Lucas, walked backward into the room pulling a mobile nurse's station which had a new IV bag of saline solution among other things. He was heavier set, but the light blue scrubs offset the look of his weight. Derrick had met him once or twice during his visits to the hospital. Corey didn't notice Derrick at first. "Oh, sorry sir, I didn't realize you were in here. I was just going to change out his IV bag and I'll be on my way. Will that be okay, or shall I bump Lucas here to the end of the list to give you more time?"

"Nah, it's fine. You can change it now. I'm not going to be able to do much today anyways."

Derrick moved aside to allow Corey ease of access to the IV line attached to Lucas's hand as well as the curled metal loop from which the old bag hung. He proceeded to scan the saline solution bag and attached it to the metal loop. Derrick rubbed his stomach; the stabbing pain was getting worse, and he assumed that getting sick was unavoidable. He moved back to his courier bag decidedly with the knowledge that nothing was going to come out of this session with Lucas. Lucas needed more time to build an awareness of Derrick, a comfort level, something repetitive and stable. Yet, the moment Derrick bent over to grab his bag, a high-pitched shriek erupted from behind him. It was enough to cause Derrick to spin on his heels grasping at his ears.

Lucas, with his eyes tightly shut and mouth over-elongated had gone into a fit. Corey had recoiled in fear and was leaning against the window along the far wall with his arms drawn up to protect his head. The sound of Lucas's wail was piercing, painful, and continuous.

"What happened?" Derrick yelled. "What'd you do?"

"Nothing! I just touched the valve on the line, and he started screaming," Corey replied, holding his ears against the shrill screech coming from Lucas.

Not stopping to even breathe, Lucas continued his howl and began shaking his head violently while flailing his arms and legs around. His body convulsed and flung backward and forward wildly.

"He's going to hurt himself!" Derrick shouted as he pressed the emergency button to the nurses' station. The IV in Lucas's arm ripped free as he thrashed about. Droplets of his blood were thrown across the room.

Corey tried to grab onto Lucas to stop his flailing, but was struck with a backhand across the nose, sending him stumbling backward and eventually to the ground. Corey's nose bled profusely down the front of his light blue scrubs. Lucas blinked his eyes uncontrollably and caught the stare of Derrick in an instant flash of consciousness before several other nurses swarmed into the room to help. Dr. Alex Leverty entered the room soon after, assessed the situation, and quickly opened one of the drawers along the back wall and removed a few disinfecting wipes. He readied a syringe. Three nurses had to hold Lucas down while Dr. Leverty cleansed an area on his arm. "Hold him still! Hold him still!" Dr. Leverty said as he lowered the syringe to administer a sedative to Lucas.

Derrick helped Corey to his feet and held a small hand towel against his bleeding nose that he had grabbed from the mobile nurses' station. Dr. Leverty continued to assist the other nurses until the sedative had taken hold of Lucas and his flailing had stopped.

In the hallway, there were several onlookers, including Dr. Evans and Detective Mitchell who had obviously heard the commotion from around the corner. A few other nurses that were concerned about the yelling came to the aid of Corey. Derrick turned to a nearby trashcan and emptied the contents of his stomach. Wiping his mouth, Derrick glanced further down the hallway, past Dr. Evans and Detective Mitchell. A nun, who apparently had been drawn to the disturbance, stood oddly expressionless as she appeared to be staring directly at Derrick. A black patch covered her right eye. Her hands were folded in front of her, and she held them by her waistline as if waiting for something, just watching.

"Derrick, what happened?" He looked at Dr. Evans and Detective Mitchell who had made their way down the hall.

"Uh, I'm not sure." Derrick peered in the direction of the nun, and she was gone. Turning his attention back to Dr. Evans, he breathed heavy. Both the detective and Dr. Evans had seen him get sick but were more concerned with the overall situation. "I don't know what happened, but Lucas is no longer catatonic." Derrick eyeballed Corey, whose nose was split open across the bridge and continued to drip through the cotton swabs that the nurses were using to stop the bleeding. "It doesn't look like he'll be going to a residency home either."

4

Friday rolled over to Saturday quickly. Outside there was a new, but light snowfall. It was early, 5:30 a.m. The temperature was still the same, bitter cold with a high of only nine degrees. Derrick sat at his desk and sipped coffee. He had carefully placed the picture of Hannah from the bedroom on his desk. She looked so happy, filled to the brim with joy. Though the picture often elicited a lament, seeing her smile still held a pleasant emotion. It also kept the thoughts of suicide away. Seeing her smile kept the gun in the drawer.

Yet the violent frenzy that Lucas displayed at the hospital sparked a new interest in Derrick, more so than the other cases he had. Similar things had manifested with children that had been horribly abused physically and sexually in the past, especially when they came across something that sparked a flashback. Fierce, aggressive outbursts were a materialization of fear, a subconscious defense mechanism. He rationalized that it was okay to dedicate more time to Lucas's case, that if he were to be any help at all he had to familiarize himself with the details. JFS wouldn't hold him accountable if he were a day or two late on visits for other case files.

To avoid Dr. Evans's scolding for his mini confrontation he had with Detective Mitchell, Derrick had spent a significant amount of time at the hospital after Lucas's outburst. He knew it was going to come in the form of a text message, where she would ask him *what the hell he was doing talking to a police officer like that.* She would ask if *he had been drinking again.* Staying to talk allowed the tension between Derrick and the detective to subside. They were able to work out a deal. Detective Mitchell was kind enough to allow Derrick to have a copy of the pertinent information from the police file to help with therapy under the agreement that any improvements made with Lucas will be reported directly to her at the police department and that communication lines needed to remain open.

The materials from the police file he had were incomplete. Derrick was only able to get copies of the crime scene photos and the initial report that was recorded which contained the background information of Lucas's parents, but nothing more. *What did you go through, Lucas? What did you have to endure?* he thought. *Acute stress disorder–PTSD–no physical marks on his body. Malnutrition–possibly neglect. Why the outburst?*

Derrick shifted his focus to the police file, specifically to a section that listed the prior offenses of Lucas's parents. They were minor offenses, misdemeanors, nothing that stood out.

Doreane Moore:

1) Misdemeanor possession of a controlled substance within Schedules II-VI (N.C.G.S. 90-95(d)(1), N.C.G.S. 90-95(d)(2), N.C.G.S. 90-95(d)(3), and N.C.G.S. 90-95(d)(4)),

2) Possession of drug paraphernalia (N.C.G.S. 90-113.22 & N.C.G.S. 90-113.24),

Ordered by the authority of Hamilton County Court to attend Crossroads Center for outpatient treatment.

Jamal Moore:
1) Misdemeanor possession of a controlled substance within Schedules II-VI (N.C.G.S. 90-95(d)(1), N.C.G.S. 90-95(d)(2), N.C.G.S. 90-95(d)(3), and N.C.G.S. 90-95(d)(4)),

Ordered by the authority of Hamilton County Court to attend Crossroads Center for outpatient treatment.

Possession of Schedule II narcotic - Oxycodone–Methamphetamine– a year ago, That's not that bad. Could've caused an anxiety disorder, I guess. Possible underlining cause of the catatonia. But what triggered the outburst yesterday? Nothing, I've got nothing. Damn! This thought played over in his mind, goading him to dig further. He laid the police report aside and reached for the photos. Brutal. Horrendously violent. Each picture represented a different angle of the bodies. Some were from across the room whereas others were closeup. Both Doreane and Jamal had their heads crushed. It looked as though each of them had had a 12-gauge shotgun blast to the back of their heads at close range, judging by the amount of damage and pooling of blood from the mangled stumps that remained as their necks. Yet, no gunpowder residue was detected nor were there any fragments of buckshot found around the scene of the crime. Below the bloody remnants of the neck the floorboards were broken downward; bits of skull were embedded into the wood; smears of gray matter were darkened by the blood and black in the dim lighting of the Moore's s apartment. Whoever committed the crime repeatedly bludgeoned their skulls until nearly nothing remained.

Disturbed by the photos, Derrick tossed them aside, grabbed the photo of his late wife, and leaned back in his chair. Absentmindedly, he sipped his coffee. It had grown cold from neglect, producing an overly bitter flavor, burnt almost. The taste was enough to cause him to seek out a fresher cup. Still clutching Hannah's picture, a chill ran the length of his body as he moved across the cold floor to the kitchen. It was more so from the mangled bodies of Lucas's parents than the actual cold from outside. *There doesn't have to be an underlining cause,* Derrick told himself. *Ferocious, the crime was just too ferocious for a ten-year-old. That's the only reason for the outburst.* Confident with this line of thought, Derrick placed Hannah's picture on the counter and poured some hot coffee. Leaving a bit of space below the rim, he reached for the bourbon and filled the remaining space in the mug. He tasted it, feeling the warmth of the coffee, with an extra sting from the bourbon. *Why would someone attack his parents in such a way? Drug dealer–nah, would've used a gun, maybe a knife, but to bludgeon– Jesus…Lucas saw it all.*

Derrick brought his coffee to his lips, sipped it again and let the aroma of the French Roast with bourbon fill his nostrils. The cold momentarily melted away and the dreadful images began to ease within his mind. He closed his eyes to enjoy the sensation, but opened them abruptly with the buzz from his cell phone. The screen read:

(513) 636-4200

It was the main line of Children's Hospital. *Debra's the only one that would call me this early*, he thought. *But why isn't she using her cell phone?*

"This is Derrick," he answered.

"Mr. Mayes–This is Detective Mitchell from the Cincinnati Police Department. I'm truly sorry to bother you at this hour, but there's been an incident here at Children's involving Lucas."

A curious anxiety started in his chest and spread throughout his body. "What kind of incident? Did he have another aggressive outburst?"

He could hear a hesitation in her voice. "Mr. Mayes, I would prefer that we talk in person. Can you come down to the hospital?"

The moment of enjoyment, the sensation that was fending off the cold and easing the horrible images of the dead bodies was broken by his *dutiful* commitment. Derrick sighed and dumped his bourbon-enhanced coffee into the sink. His voice was thick with apprehension. "Yeah. Give me at least a half-hour."

5

Despite saying a half-hour to Detective Mitchell, it took Derrick nearly forty-five minutes to make himself presentable and arrive at the hospital. A few police cruisers were parked outside the main entrance of the building. Inside, there was a different feeling, it was more grim than prior days. Even Dorothy behind the information desk was without a smile, appearing somber. A twinge of nausea stirred in Derrick's stomach. Acid forced its way up and caused him to burp. Coffee mostly, but with a hint of bourbon.

"Mr. Mayes." Derrick glanced passed the information desk at Detective Mitchell who was walking toward him. She appeared tired, less composed than she did on the previous meeting. Perhaps it was because she wasn't buttoned to the brim with a formal coat. Or that her suit jacket was open, revealing a loose-fitting blouse. Derrick wagered she was about his age but wasn't going to make a point of it. "Mr. Mayes. Thank you for coming down here on such short notice. I know that you're busy and this is an inconvenience, but I wouldn't have called if it wasn't of the utmost importance."

Detective Mitchell lacked her jovial demeanor and wasn't trying to keep up professional pretenses. Her tone was grave, but direct. Derrick's stomach continued to churn and twist with acid. "You mentioned this involved Lucas. Did he hurt himself or someone else?"

"No, not at all. Mr. Mayes–"

"Derrick, my name is Derrick."

"Very well, Derrick. Can we talk in private?"

"Yeah, sure."

Derrick held back the ill feeling in his stomach as he followed Detective Mitchell down the hall to a waiting area that was sectioned off by the police and was being used as a space to conduct police business. Dr. Evans sat on one of the green chairs resting her elbows on her knees and holding a cup of coffee with both hands. Tears dripped down her cheeks amongst a saddened expression. "Debra? What's wrong? What happened?"

Dr. Evans looked up at Derrick, placed her coffee on the floor next to her seat, and immediately embraced him in a hug. Detective Mitchell stood close by without saying anything.

"He's gone," she said between heavy sobs.

"Who's gone? What are you talking about?"

"Alex, Dr. Leverty." Dr. Evans continued to sob, leaning her head on Derrick's shoulder.

"A custodian found him a little after 3:00 a.m." Detective Mitchell interjected. "Blood had seeped out from behind a medical closet door on the first floor just around the corner."

"I'm sorry, I don't follow." Derrick's confusion was genuine as he oscillated his head between the detective and Dr. Evans.

"Dr. Leverty was killed last night. We're certainly suspecting foul play." Detective Mitchell was back to studying Derrick with her eyes. They were sharp, bold, and unforgiving with their inquisitiveness.

"He was murdered? How–I mean…I don't get–"

"Dr. Leverty…had his heart ripped out of his chest," Detective Mitchell said. Dr. Evans gasped, her face contorted, lips trembled into a weep when the detective revealed this information. The detective's voice was controlled, but purposeful, and paid no attention to Dr. Evans. She remained fixated on Derrick, studying him, examining his reaction.

Another acidy burp made its way up Derrick's throat. He brought his hand to his mouth to help conceal it and turned away from the detective. The thought of Dr. Leverty having his heart torn from his chest was repulsive.

"I don't get it," Derrick said turning back to the detective. "Why did you call me down here? What's this have to do with Lucas?"

The detective pursed her lips, clearly analyzing Derrick's reaction, but accepting the fact that it revealed nothing more than what she already suspected. "Dr. Leverty was seen on the security footage entering the medical closet, but never came out. As I had mentioned, he was found by the custodial staff because the blood had poured onto the floor and ran under the door. Dr. Leverty had visited Lucas's room approximately twenty-five minutes prior to his death according to his log. We would like to question Lucas, but since he is under the custody of JFS and you're his case worker, we need your permission to do so."

"I don't know if that's a good idea. I mean you both were here when he had his outburst yesterday. He may not be ready, no–he's *not* ready for that kind of questioning."

"Derrick, this murder has the same grisly signature as Lucas's parents."

"Oh, come on, you don't think that Lucas–"

"No, not at all. A child couldn't kill in such a way. Dr. Leverty's heart was torn out from the back. A hole was punched directly through the muscles. Bones were broken inward, and the heart was literally twisted from the chest cavity. This was done by someone very sadistic and strong." Dr. Evans backed away from Derrick, covered her face with her hand, and let her heavy sobs freely flow. Detective Mitchell glanced at her briefly before returning her gaze to Derrick. "This also suggests that the person may be stalking Lucas in some strange manner. As of right now, he's our only connection to both murders."

"Still, questioning a child that has gone through his kind of trauma will surely elicit a bad reaction. Come on Debra, tell her."

Dr. Evans had sat back down on the green chair and proceeded to stare at the floor, shaking her head, crying, and mumbling. "Who could do such a thing? He had a family, a wife...children." She looked up at Derrick. "I don't get it."

"Derrick you're a therapist."

"*Was* a therapist," Derrick corrected the detective.

"My point is, you have training. If we can't question him, you can. Please Derrick, we need to know if there was anyone else with Dr. Leverty when he came into Lucas's room. Or if Lucas noticed anything strange, out of the ordinary, anything."

Derrick placed his hands on his hips and shook his head, considering everything that the detective had mentioned. "Trust me, this is *not* going to go well."

"We have to try."

Derrick said nothing more. Instead, he waved his hand in a *'whatever'* gesture and made his way to the elevator. Detective Mitchell followed closely behind. Dr. Evans said she was too distraught to be involved at this point and elected to stay behind. As they both waited for the doors of the elevator to open, a swarm of police officers and members of the forensic team to their left were still photographing the scene of the crime, dusting for prints, and tending to the area. Derrick could see a pool of blood that extended far into the hallway. It had more than just poured from under the door. With a welcomed ding and distraction from the horrific scene a little way down the hall, the doors to the elevator opened.

The sick feeling bubbled inside Derrick, to a point where he almost needed a nearby trashcan again. He took several deep breaths in the elevator, hoping to quell the feeling but more so that Detective Mitchell would not suspect he was incompetent with his duties, especially since he tasted the bourbon each time he burped. Even the Shea butter lotion he used to conceal the alcohol smell at times could not conceal a physical illness.

"Are you all right, Derrick?" The detective had clued into his heavy breathing.

"Yeah. I'm fine. It just–I'm not a police officer and cases–like this–"

"Are unsettling." Detective Mitchell finished his statement, showing a little more compassion for the situation with her interruption.

Seizing the opportunity to cover his stomach ailment, Derrick nodded. "Yeah, unsettling."

The elevator doors opened with a ding to a brightly lit hallway full of color. It did nothing to quell the melancholy aura that had permeated the building. Derrick could feel it in the air and see it on those that were still trying to execute their duties to care for the children. There was an absence on the floor; a void that was affecting everyone. Lucas's room was a few doors down the hall on the right. A uniformed officer sat in a chair just outside the door. It was standard for the Cincinnati Police Department to station someone next to the room when there was a patient that was involved with something heavy like murder. Both Detective Mitchell and Derrick stopped at the door. The uniformed officer only acknowledged Detective Mitchell and very astutely listened when she motioned that it was okay for him to leave. It was as though Derrick didn't even exist to him, which was a point that Derrick didn't belabor. It was one less person he had to interact with and given the state of his stomach, this was certainly a positive thing.

Derrick sighed and unbuttoned his coat. "I don't mind if you stay out here and listen in of course, but I do need to speak with him alone to establish trust. Our last meeting didn't go over too well."

Detective Mitchell understood and removed a small notepad from inside her suit coat. She stayed back as Derrick entered the room. Lucas was sitting straight up in his bed staring directly at the wall in front of him. Upon Derrick's entering the room, his head slowly shifted. His eyes were bright, alert and caught Derrick in a stare similar to that of Detective Mitchell. Catatonia had clearly dissipated.

"Good morning, Lucas. Do you remember who I am?" Lucas said nothing in return, but continued to stare, unflinching. His face was expressionless, yet he was aware of his surroundings. "I was hoping we would be able to talk today. Would you be okay with that?"

Lucas tilted his head slightly as Derrick sat down in one of the cushioned chairs in the room and removed a notepad from his courier bag and let it gently slide off his shoulder to the floor. The bubbling and churning in Derrick's stomach hadn't subsided. It caused him to feel clammy. Sweat formed across his upper lip and brow. Lucas's stare was piercing, but he remained silent.

"Are you feeling okay today?" Derrick asked. No response from Lucas. "Lucas, I want you to know that I'm a friend. I'm going to help you." Lucas was stoic. "Do you know Dr. Evans? She's a friend of mine and has also been looking after you ever since you first came here." No response from Lucas. Derrick noted each time he asked a question and received no response. "Dr. Leverty is a friend of mine too. Do you know who he is?" Lucas tilted his head slightly but spoke no words. Derrick was keen to note the subtle change. "He was one of the doctors that checked-in on you last night. Did you know that? You may have been asleep." Lucas tilted his head the opposite direction and Derrick made a note again. Dr. Leverty's name elicited a response, no matter how small it was. Derrick continued his line of questioning. "You remember him coming into your room last night?" Derrick didn't wait for the response. "Was he the only one you remember coming into your room last night? Do you remember anyone else?"

Lucas merely blinked, remained silent, but provided no other response or tilts of the head. Derrick took in a deep breath realizing that this was probably the best that he was going to get out of Lucas. Acid bubbled in his throat and Derrick let out another burp. He covered his mouth and turned away from Lucas. Immediately he made note of where the nearest trashcan was in case he had to reach for it. He burped again.

"Bour-bon."

Derrick's head snapped forward catching Lucas's stare. "Did you say something Lucas?" Derrick had heard him but needed confirmation. "What did you say? Say that again Lucas."

He remained quiet, not indulging in the request. A slight smirk had appeared. Derrick attempted to make a note of the change. However, a knot-like gnawing pain erupted inside Derrick's stomach forcing him to stop.

He grabbed at his abdomen. Gut rot from drinking too much is what it resembled, yet it had the intensity of stomach flu with the cramping and twisting. Sweat from his upper lip and brow began to drip down his face onto his neck. Lucas stayed fixed on Derrick, unflinching. His eyes followed Derrick as he reached for his bag and made his way toward the hospital room door.

Detective Mitchell was still standing in the hallway outside the door, still holding her notepad. She had recorded all the questions that she heard Derrick ask while he was in the room. Derrick moved past her and found a small trashcan below one of the computer alcoves in the hall. He brought it to his chest and proceeded to get sick the same as the last time. Cockroaches scurried out from underneath the tissues and other bits of paper garbage that was in the small trashcan. Immediately, Derrick dropped it to the floor. He waited for the roaches to run out onto the floor, but none did.

"Are you all right Derrick?" Detective Mitchell asked as she moved closer to his side.

"I think I'm coming down with a stomach bug or something." Derrick was momentarily distracted from the trashcan as he noticed the detective glancing around to see if anyone had heard what Derrick had said. She knew as well as Derrick that if he had indeed come down with a stomach ailment that he would *not* be allowed back on the floor again until he showed no signs of the contagion. That could drastically hinder an investigation.

"Derrick, have you been drinking?" Her question was insightful, yet still held the same level of directness that most of her questions bore.

"What makes you say that?" Derrick said as he took one last glimpse at the trashcan to see if the roaches were inside. No bugs.

"Derrick, I don't care if you were drinking last night or even the other time that you came to the hospital. You're a grown man. However, I'm a homicide detective and I need to know that you're not going to hinder my investigation."

Breathing heavy, "I'm–I'm better now," Derrick stated quickly. It wasn't a total lie, but it wasn't the total truth either.

Detective Mitchell nodded, her eyes still suggesting disbelief. "Okay then. I heard the questions you asked. Were there any responses?"

Derrick wiped his mouth and took a couple of deep breaths. "Only tilts of the head."

"I don't follow."

"When I brought up Dr. Leverty's name, the only response that Lucas gave was a slight tilt of the head."

"So, what does that mean?"

Derrick continued to take deep breaths. "Nothing really. Maybe that he remembers him being in the room, but that's not anything we didn't already know."

"Was there anything else that Lucas did or even said that was different?"

Derrick thought for a moment. He knew that Lucas had uttered the word *bourbon,* but he wasn't going to tell the detective this. How or why Lucas chose that word was still beyond him. Detective Mitchell was already questioning if he was infringing upon the investigation. Certainly, if he were to divulge the utterance, he would be removed from the case, but more so would run the risk of being fired from JFS. As much as he had grown to hate the position, he needed it. "No…he said nothing."

Again, Detective Mitchell paused for a moment, then merely nodded and motioned with her head for Derrick to follow her back to the elevator. One of the on-duty nurses had seen Derrick get sick and discretely came over with latex gloves on and offered to take the soiled trashcan. Out of the corner of Derrick's eye, he noticed a familiar figure standing further down the hallway again. It was the same nun he had seen before. Same patch across her right eye, poised in the same expectant manner with her hands folded in front of her. She stood out, but no one else seemed to care except Derrick. He looked back at Detective Mitchell who was waiting at the elevator door, holding it open for him. At second glance toward the nun, she was gone, again. A recognizable chill started on the nape of Derrick's neck and ran the length of his spine forcing a shiver.

6

It was not long after returning to the first floor that Derrick started to feel better. The cramping, gnawing pain in his stomach had subsided and though he was hungry, the queasiness had almost dissipated. He draped his coat over the armrest of the chair next to him. Detective Mitchell brought Derrick a cup of coffee.

"Thank you." He grasped the paper cup with both hands and sipped it gently. "May I work here for a little while?" Derrick asked as he looked around the waiting area space the police had sectioned off.

"Yes of course. Are you feeling better?" she asked as she sat next to Derrick on one of the cushioned chairs.

Derrick nodded. "Yu–up...I think it was mostly nerves."

"Derrick, if it's alcohol–stop now. We need your help."

His eyes met the detective's. If he didn't have to admit anything, he wasn't going to. "Nerves detective–nerves."

Not satisfied with the answer by her trademark pursing of the lips, Detective Mitchell nonetheless accepted the response and pushed the issue no further. Yet, there was a mutual understanding between them that should Derrick become sick in her presence again, he would be removed as the JFS worker for Lucas's case. She stood and looked around before glancing back down at Derrick. "Well…I'll leave you to your work." She shook a finger at him as if wanting to say more. Instead, she turned from Derrick and continued to manage the other police officers that were swarming about tending to their duties. Derrick looked around hoping to see Dr. Evans, but she had gone. He pulled out his cell phone. The lock screen read:

1 missed call and voicemail

Derrick hoped it was from Dr. Evans and swiped the screen to listen to the message, not fully paying attention to the number.

Message one received Saturday, January twelfth at seven fifteen a.m. Mr. Mayes…this is Mary Ellen Ferguson calling again about Jeremiah. I don't know what you think you are doing, but this has become very unprofessional. I have been approved by the agency and the courts to be the legal foster parent and guardian of Jeremiah. The only hold-up is you. If this does not get expedited, I am placing a call to your agency about your lack of attention to your work with Jeremiah…

Derrick deleted the message. *Bitch,* he thought. *If she only knew what was happening.* With the lack of a family to adopt Jeremiah, Derrick knew that he would have to bite the bullet and complete the processing for Mary Ellen. Her constant nagging presence was an irritant, whether it was in person or in a voicemail. It didn't matter. Derrick was more concerned about Dr. Evans than Mary Ellen. He tapped his text message icon and then tapped Dr. Evans's name in the queue.

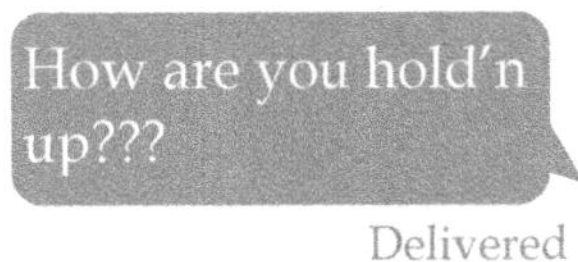

Delivered

Derrick waited a moment to see if she would respond. Nothing. *Damn! She's gotta be a mess. I'll call her when I leave here*, Derrick thought.

Tossing his phone onto the folds of his coat, he reached into his courier bag and pulled out his Chromebook. He shifted in his seat and rested the small computer on his legs as he waited for it to boot up. People were buzzing all around him. The same aura of dismay also permeated the first floor. It affected the whole building. Portions of the hospital were locked down and uniformed police officers could be seen at the end of each hallway. No one seemed willing to smile, nor should they. A prominent doctor within the building had been brutally murdered by someone. As far as the police were concerned that person could be anyone and could be anywhere. Their only connection was Lucas.

Derrick's computer booted up with a chime. He clicked on the icon to open his daily log for JFS.

Log: January 12th, 2019

I met with a newer file today: Case ONE: Previously diagnosed with Catatonia suspected to be brought on by Acute Stress Disorder and/or PTSD. 10-year-old African American boy had been in this state since his arrival at Children's Hospital until a violent outburst on Friday, January 11th where the file seemingly experienced a flashback that sent him into an uncontrollable fit which resulted in sedation. Attending physicians are Dr. Debra Evans and was Dr. Alex Leverty. I was called to the hospital at 5:30 a.m. and arrived at 6:15 a.m. under the impression that the boy had been harmed or had harmed another person with another violent outburst. Upon arrival at the hospital, I came to find that Dr. Alex Leverty had been murdered and the young boy was on his list of patients that he had visited prior to his death. With the heavy police involvement and being that JFS has custody, I was solicited to question the boy to determine if there was someone other than Dr. Leverty that had come into the room.

Derrick stopped typing at the sound of a text message on his phone. He grabbed it and slid the lock screen. It was from Dr. Evans:

I'll be alright…

Derrick could see that she was texting another message. He gave it another moment. It still showed that she was typing. *Unless she's typing a long response, she probably accidentally typed a letter*, he thought. Not overly concerned, Derrick went back to his log.

Upon entering the room of the boy, he was sitting up in his bed and made direct eye contact with me as I walked further in. This supports the claim that the catatonic state was over. The child remained silent throughout the duration of my questions, merely tilting his head to one side at the mention of Dr. Leverty.

Derrick stopped typing again as he heard his cell ding with another text message. He swiped the lock screen. It was from Dr. Evans again.

I'll be alright…

If you fuck me in
the ass!!!!

Derrick did a double-take at the message sent by Dr. Evans. *What the fuck?* he thought. Without warning his phone exploded with text messages all reading the same as the previous message. Confused, Derrick assumed that the messages were some kind of glitch. Scrambling, he attempted to turn off his phone, but it wouldn't respond. The messages continued to pour into his phone.

"What the hell? What the hell?" Derrick whispered in a mild panic.

From his Chromebook, he heard sexual moaning. Derrick glanced down to see a browser window had been opened and was playing a particularly vulgar pornographic movie. The volume of the video was steadily increasing and the moaning was getting louder and louder. Like his cell phone, the computer was not responding to the manual volume controls, and he was unable to close out the browser window. Even more panicked, Derrick looked around to see if anyone had noticed the vulgar sounds coming from his computer. People from across the hall appeared to be looking at him and contorting their faces in a disgusted fashion. Sweat formed across his brow and upper lip the same as it had done before. His breathing intensified. Thumps from his heart echoed in his ears. Whispers emerged from everywhere and nowhere, overlapping simultaneously. *"Oh my God, he's watching porn in a hospital! That's disgusting! Perverted fuck! What's he doing?"* Desperate, Derrick pressed *ctrl–alt–delete* to end the task, but that too seemed to fail. For a brief moment, Derrick clued into the video. The male stud was an African American with his back to the camera, and the woman who was dressed in black leather with various openings for sexual play looked an awful lot like Dr. Evans. The woman was also screaming Derrick's name. *"Oh Derrick! Fuck me Derrick! Fuck me in the ass! Fuck me!"*

"Excuse me." Derrick slammed shut his Chromebook, still breathing heavy from panic. Standing before him was an elderly woman, a nun, the same nun he had seen twice before on Lucas's floor. The dreadful sexual moaning sounds from his computer had stopped as did the whispers. Derrick glanced at his phone and the vulgar messages from Dr. Evans weren't there. Only the message, *I'll be alright…* remained on his text message queue. No one was looking at him with contorted faces. In fact, no one seemed to notice he was even there except for the nun. Derrick stared around in bewilderment. He glanced back at her as she spoke again. "Excuse me. I didn't mean to startle you."

Her voice was raspy, stern. She was not wearing her habit as she was before, and her hair was in no particular order. It matched her wrinkled, weathered face. "No–no it's just–I was distracted by something else."

Slowly, Derrick wiped the sweat from his forehead.

"My name is Sister Christina and I know what's distracting you, Mr. Derrick Mayes."

"I'm sorry who are you?" Derrick asked, more cautious of the nun at the mention of his name. Her one good eye was piercing, brown, beady-like, with a keen focus.

"As I have already stated, I'm Sister Christina." She sat down next to Derrick. "I understand that you are the JFS caseworker for the child in room 414?"

"Sister, I don't know how you know me, and I guess it doesn't really matter, but under HIPPA I cannot acknowledge or deny that any of the cases I work on are under the custody of JFS. If you wish to speak with me about any particular case that JFS manages, you'll have to provide a written consent form from an authorizing body."

"God is my authorizing body, Mr. Mayes. But I'm also respectful of the law and understand that I'm not allowed to visit your client without your approval."

"Well, God has nothing to do with the laws concerning case management or JFS. I've stated my position already, Sister. Unless you have a consent form, I'm not authorized to talk with you about any cases I have. Now if you'll excuse me, as *I* have already stated, I'm a bit distracted at the moment." Derrick stood, secured his Chromebook in his courier bag, and put on his coat. He slid his phone into the interior pocket. Sister Christina simply watched with her beady eye; her face ostensibly lacking in expression. "Excuse me," Derrick said turning from the nun.

"It's not going to stop Mr. Mayes…your distraction." Derrick paused a little way into the hall that led out of the hospital. He glanced over his shoulder toward the nun. "It's only going to get worse," she finished.

Derrick turned from her shaking his head and left the hospital.

7

It was nearly 11:00 a.m. before Derrick got back to his apartment. He shook off the bitter frost as he stepped inside. Yet, the strangeness of the morning kept an icy chill in his mind. Something was wrong, very wrong. Murder had stretched its fingers into a place of healing. Why? Why target a psychiatric pediatrician? Though he didn't know Dr. Alex Leverty as well as Dr. Evans, the way he died was enough to upset the balance in anyone's day. Whether or not it had an effect on Lucas was too early to tell, but his behavior was equally as odd. *I know he said bourbon. How the hell did he know what I was drinking?* He swiped his phone from the lock screen and double-checked the text message queue. The paroxysm of the same text message that had seemingly come from Dr. Evans was non-existent as if somebody had erased them or as if they weren't even there in the first place.

Derrick laid his phone down on one of the end tables in his living room. *Think, think! You're a therapist! You've seen this stuff before! Alcohol. It must be from the drinking,* Derrick told himself. *The porn. I never watch porn on the Chromebook. How? Nerves, you threw up, again. It's gotta be your nerves. Depression maybe. Does funny things to the mind.* Derrick continued to rack his brain for answers, but came up with only a firm grasp on nothing. He sat in one of his living room chairs and pulled his Chromebook from his courier bag. After the disruption from the batty old nun, Derrick didn't have an opportunity to explore how the porno movie suddenly began playing. Nor was he able to rationalize the whispers. They came from everywhere and nowhere at the same time. It was as if the people around him were whispering, disgusted by him, by his porn addiction. But, none of it was real and no browser windows had been opened on his computer, only his daily log. How it happened baffled Derrick. Even rationalizing alcohol as a source of the strangeness was inappropriate; it didn't match. None of it matched. "What's happening to me," he whispered. "Is this how it happens with people? Am I losing it? No…depression, just nerves."

Derrick resolved to leave Lucas's case alone for the rest of the day and considered not going back to the hospital until Dr. Evans communicated a change in his status. The case had grown heavy, quickly and Derrick needed to attend to his other files as well, especially Mary Ellen breathing down his neck about Jeremiah. Falling behind as a case worker could be disastrous and would likely lead to a hole that could take months to climb out of. He needed to be of sound mind. A mental breakdown was simply an inconvenience, at best.

Switching his focus back to his other cases, Derrick decided that he would review the case files, make a few calls, and maybe even go out on a visit to the West Side. As much as he loathed driving all the way out to the West Side, he knew it would be the right kind of distraction from Lucas's case. Many of the JFS workers took Saturday evenings off unless they were on-call. Yet, ever since Hannah died, Saturday evenings proved to be invaluable for catching up on missed appointments and visits from the earlier parts of the week. Derrick didn't have anything that was tying him to home. Often, these Saturday visits would also provide insights into the family structures that surrounded the children he served. It wasn't unheard of to catch a drunken abuse situation or even see the home environment outside of the weekly routine that people tend to follow Monday through Friday. At the very least, he was less likely to get no-showed.

The clock on the cable box read 11:30 a.m. Derrick closed his Chromebook and set it on the coffee table in front of him. Being up early as well as the nature of the events that had unfolded since Derrick woke, fatigue was present. He leaned back in the cushioned chair and propped his feet up on the ottoman. His mind was swimming with questions and confusion. Pictures of him and Hannah filled the wall space. Most were candid pics that turned out cute, nothing professional. They were sentimental moments of short trips together around the state or just over the river into Northern Kentucky. He missed that the most. The intimate moments that were nothing to anyone other than he and Hannah. Drowsy, blurry from weariness, Derrick closed his eyes allowing the images of Hannah to swirl around inside his head. A strange guilt consumed him. It was an empty guilt, as though the plug had been pulled on the remaining emotions he had inside leaving behind only self-reproach. He couldn't relax, no matter how hard he tried. His body was in a state of rebellion. No way was he going to be able to work on the other files in this condition.

Though an ambitious thought, sleep was a more logical, immediate distraction. *The other files can wait an hour. After a drink and nap,* he thought. Derrick strolled over to the kitchen. A rocks glass was already sitting on the counter near the bourbon. No need for ice, just bourbon. The bottle was nearly half empty. He poured. Something shifted in Derrick's mind as if things around him began to slow. Through the glass, Derrick caught a glimpse of his late wife's picture that he had left there earlier. It was oddly different through the bottle and the bourbon that sloshed back and forth. Instead of a warm, jovial smile, Hannah's face was contorted into an angry, painful expression. Eyebrows furrowed down and inward, a clenching of the jaw and eyes that deeply penetrated. Dropping the bottle, Derrick closed his eyes tightly not concerned about the spillage of bourbon. He placed both hands on the countertop. "Guilt...guilt manifests like this. Just breathe, breathe."

His heartbeat grew louder in his ears as the adrenaline pulsed through his body. Anxiety flooded his chest making each breath harder to take. Sweat formed again on his face. Clammy, sick to his stomach, Derrick felt faint. *"I'm here Derrick...we're here...over here..."* Derrick opened his eyes and spun on his heels as a whoosh of air passed over the back of his neck and carried a whisper that faded and overlapped with others. A chill spread throughout the small kitchen.

"What the fuck?" Derrick muttered between labored breaths of panic.

"Heeeee-rrre!" came another breath of air and a whisper drawing Derrick's attention back to the photo of his late wife on the counter. Her expression had changed again to a lustful anger and her eyes had turned iridescent materializing into a sinister ruddiness that wasn't quite red, yet fiery nonetheless. With both hands, he grasped the photo frame and drew it close, disbelieving his own senses. The whispers continued. *"Addict…liar…suicide…come join us Derrick…do it…"*

"STOP IT! THIS ISN'T REAL!" Derrick yelled, feeling the room spinning. His eyes were locked on the photo, terrified, but unable to look away. The mouth of his wife elongated and brought forth a shriek that came from a distance and arrived with piercing clarity. Cockroaches ran across the edge of the wood frame and down the front of the glass over his wife's face and onto his hands. "STOOOOP!"

BANG, BANG, BANG!

The room came into focus and Derrick dropped the picture frame. It crashed to the floor of his kitchen, shattering the glass. The expression of his late wife had gone back to its happy, jovial state as if nothing had happened. There were no roaches either. Barely able to catch his breath, Derrick fell to his knees. Tears escaped his eyes and mixed with sweat that rolled down his cheeks.

BANG, BANG, BANG!

Someone was at the door. Derrick forced himself to stand. Wobbly, he leaned against the counter for a moment to gain his composure. He wiped the sweat and tears off his face with his sleeve. Around his apartment, everything seemed normal. "What the hell? What the hell?" he said as he took a couple of long, deep breaths.

Still wobbly, Derrick moved toward the door. Through the peephole, he couldn't tell who it was. The person was standing with her back to the door, only allowing the backside of her head to be visible. Cautiously, he opened the door a crack, just enough to peer out.

Breathing hard. "Can–can I help you?"

Turning to catch Derrick's gaze was a familiar face, though not a pleasant one. "Mr. Mayes," a stern, gravelly voice stated.

"Seriously? You're kidding me?" He opened the door wider. A feeling of frustration brought a sense of life back into Derrick. Rational thought returned and most of the ill feelings that had been present only moments before had dissipated. Standing before him, cheeks rosy from the wintry weather with one eye covered under a black patch was the elderly nun, Sister Christina.

8.

Derrick stared directly at the nun. She must've followed him from the hospital. It was lunacy. It was illegal. "What are you doing here?" Derrick spat at her.

The nun's expression remained austere. She studied Derrick's state before she sighed strong and deep. "It's already begun. I know what's happening to you, Mr. Mayes. We really should talk inside."

"With all due respect, Sister, I'm tired. I'm not in a sound state right now and the fact that you followed me from the hospital…" Derrick stopped his statement and cocked his head to one side to suggest the strangeness of the situation without saying outright.

"No, Mr. Mayes. It's more than just being tired."

"You know the police feel that the murder at the hospital last night is linked to two other murders that happened earlier this week. Both are overly brutal. They feel that the murderer has been stalking the victims that surround a child. How do I know that you're not that person?"

"Do I look like the type that would harm anyone as grotesquely as Dr. Leverty or the parents of Lucas, Doreane, and Jamal Moore?" Though thrown by the amount of information she was able to speak on and the strangeness of her very presence, the foolishness of Derrick's implication that she could be the murderer set in the moment after Sister Christina casually pointed it out. *This was done by someone very sadistic and strong.* Detective Mitchell's words echoed in Derrick's thoughts. Frail, not strong was her appearance. "You've had hallucinations, haven't you?" she asked abruptly. "I heard the screams from outside."

The question also caught Derrick off-guard. How could she know what just happened? "Who are you? How do you know all this about me, Lucas, Dr. Leverty?"

"Being in *its* presence brings out the worst in us. I'm someone who's gone through what you're experiencing. And I've been following in its deathly wake ever since." Sister Christina paused before she continued. "We should talk inside," she urged again.

Derrick shifted uncomfortably in the doorway. The wind blew strong from outside carrying a chilling bite. Snow swirled through the corridor of the apartment complex. The nun seemed immune to it. Her silvery hair blew wildly, yet she remained indifferent, unflinching. There was something deeper to her, though. Below the hardened, weathered exterior Derrick could see emotions, remnants of painful ones: loss, remorse, emotions of torment. They showed on the lines of her face, but the depth came from the look in her eye. Hollow, barren yet reflective of a lament. Derrick knew that look well. It was one brought on by pain, a special kind of pain. The pain of realizing that the life aspired to was merely a fallacy, a pretend, propaganda image of a prescribed life. Not from a failure once or even twice but from the blackened abyss of loneliness, sustained over time.

Derrick opened the door fully and allowed Sister Christina to come inside. "Thank you," she said.

Once inside Derrick made his way back into the kitchen where he had dropped the picture of his late wife. He didn't care all that much about being civil with the nun. Upon re-entering the kitchen, he threw a dish towel on top of the spilled bourbon. To the left of the refrigerator were a broom and a small dustpan. All he wanted to do was get the shattered glass off the floor and remove the picture from the broken frame, which he placed on the counter behind him. Fortunately, most of the glass was in large pieces. Easy to clean. Derrick still made a full sweep of the floor to catch the smaller, grain-like pieces that would be quite unpleasant to step on barefooted. He finished and placed the broom back in its spot. Derrick turned to find Sister Christina standing at the edge of the kitchen with the photo of Hannah in her hands. A twinge of angst raced through Derrick. "What are you doing?" he asked casually, but direct.

"This is how *it* attacks. It strikes at the very things we care about the most, but it uses the worst parts of us as weapons."

"I don't know what is happening here, but specifics. In my line of work, we deal with specifics. You keep referring to *it*. Are you going to tell me what *it* is and how *it* pertains to me? Why you're here, perhaps?"

Sister Christina laid the photo back down on the counter. "Shall we sit?" The nun motioned with her hand to the living room.

"After you." Derrick's voice carried a cautious tenor, yet he followed the nun into the living room. He sat in one of the cushioned chairs and she sat on the couch across from him. Sister Christina removed a satchel that was draped across her torso. Derrick hadn't noticed it when she was standing in the doorway. She laid the bag flat and removed a file from it.

"I shall be frank. *It*…is a demon."

"A what?"

"A demon, Mr. Mayes." Her voice had a touch of sarcasm, yet still implied an obvious truth that Derrick was missing. "I'm convinced that the child you're servicing at Children's is tormented by this demon and that you too are being affected. You're a drinker, Mr. Mayes, right?"

"I'm surprised that you know that, but do I dare ask how?"

"I watched you get sick in the hospital, twice. Like I said, the demon brings out the worst in us when we are simply around it. Drinking too much makes us sick, so the demon has been drawing it out of you at inopportune times. You can call it a *defense mechanism* if you like, but it's also a form of attack. With you providing services to Lucas, the body *it* has inhabited, is drawing too much attention. So, it's going to attack you in ways that'll get you into trouble and delay your work. It's *selective* with whom it torments."

"Okay stop! You're expecting me to believe that my sleep-deprived, stress-induced manifestations of the mind, even my episodes of illness that truly can be attributed to alcohol are in fact being caused by a demon possessing a child?" Disbelief poured from Derrick's mouth. "Anxiety is a better diagnosis. I've seen it hundreds of times in clients I've treated. Too much of the bad hormones, like cortisol that upset the body's homeostasis, can cause very adverse reactions to simple things as well as manifest into dementia, nightmares, insomnia, chronic fatigue syndrome, depression, and the list goes on." Derrick paused for a moment to reflect on what he was about to say. "My wife died two years ago, and I haven't adjusted well to it. That's all. Perhaps I should talk to someone about it, instead of drinking. But to say that a demon is causing this…come on, how can I believe that?"

"Of course, you don't," she said with a heavy sigh of indifference. Sister Christina pursed her lips and nodded her head. She opened the file she had taken out of the satchel. "It wants you to believe that. It wants you to go insane thinking about what *it* could be. The more you are distracted the easier it becomes for it to carry out its work. The child, Lucas, is its instrument." Sister Christina laid the file upon the coffee table in front of the couch and began removing newspaper clippings and photos from it.

The blatant disregard for his explanation annoyed Derrick. This rational line of thinking had serviced him well over the years and had assisted with the treatment of hundreds of children. Not only did he not like it when others dipped into cases that he had, especially when they weren't authorized, but dismissing his expertise was simply an insult. "I'm not going to ask how you came about acquiring the information you have about Lucas, but I can assure you that it's illegal to do what you're doing. I'll have to file a report on this and there may be further police involvement."

"You must do what you feel is right, of course, but as I mentioned at the hospital, God is my authorizing body. Protecting the confidentiality of Lucas is noble and to be expected from a person that holds your position, but foolish. The facts of the matter are that *it* kills. I've come to know that it uses children to carry out its evil deeds."

"Kills? Me being foolish? Huh! Really…I mean who does *it* target?" Derrick asked. His voice was laced with skepticism. This was starting to sound an awful lot like a case he had a few years ago with a child that was physically abused. The case involved a grandmother who was heating a small, silver crucifix and forcing her granddaughter to hold the scalding metal in her hand so that she could feel the burning pain that Christ would bring upon those that consorted with the devil. Having done this so much, the child had a permanent scar in the shape of a crucifix on her palm. This act of abuse was brought on by the fact that the grandmother found a pop culture teen magazine in the child's room that had a picture of Josh Hutcherson in a t-shirt that showed off his arm muscles. When asked about the abuse, the grandmother stated and truly believed that the child was possessed.

"Sinners, Mr. Mayes. The demon targets sinners." The nun began lying down in a linear order the photos she was removing from the file. Each one was a horrendous murder of some kind. Pictures of people with their hands and feet severed, throats torn completely out exposing the interior of the trachea, disembowelments, crushed skulls, and various other pictures of the human body in poses of extreme death. "Each of these people had committed some form of taboo. After each of their deaths the news reports often revealed the foul things they had been involved with; things like child pornography, rape, and other sexual offenses, even murder, you name it. Their sins called this demon forth." Sister Christina laid several newspaper clippings on top of the photos in front of Derrick.

"Alright, I get it, there are a lot of very sick people in this world, but you're starting to sound like the pastor at my mother's church. You can't even talk to the man without hell and damnation and the devil spilling from his lips. It's *why* I don't go there anymore!" Derrick's voice began to rise in irritation. "No one seems to take into account psychology, mental illness, and the things that the body can do when stressed in a wrong fashion. Come on, you've been around a while, you seem smart, resourceful, even cunning; you have to see this from my perspective."

Derrick stood from the chair and walked back toward the kitchen. Bourbon. He still needed a drink to calm his nerves. "Drinking won't make it go away, Mr. Mayes," Sister Christina flatly stated.

Derrick faced her. "Maybe not, but right now it's what I need. This is too much. In fact, this is insane! You illegally dip into a case that I am working on and request to see the child. When I refuse in a professional, legal fashion you continued to *illegally* dig for information at the hospital, then you follow me home, and try to convince me that a demon is making me sick and causing me to hallucinate. Furthermore, you state that the demon is using the child to kill…no, not just kill, brutally mutilate bodies whom you claim to be *sinners*. You include Dr. Leverty, a psychiatric pediatrician, with a wife and children, who worked to heal other children every day to be part of this *sinner* group. You have to be *fucking* kidding me! This stupid shit is exactly why I stopped going to church! Why I stopped listening!"

He turned away from Sister Christina, grabbed the bottle of bourbon that was lying on its side, and began to pour it into the rocks glass. Most of the liquor was sopped up from the dish towel where it had spilled out onto the counter. Enough remained for a stiff drink, maybe two if needed.

"Do you hear the whispers, Mr. Mayes?" Her voice was cold, direct. Derrick stopped pouring the liquor and froze. He felt his pulse quicken and his breathing become more labored. "Do they taunt you? Do they reveal your secrets, your vices, the things you do when no one else is around? You heard them at the hospital earlier today. I could see the panic on your face." A lump formed in Derrick's throat, making it hard to swallow. "Dr. Leverty may have appeared just, noble, even family-oriented, but neither of us knows what lay beneath the veil he wore. Just as you appear to the world, you have openly stated you have a drinking problem, that you haven't handled your wife's death well. What other vices do you have, Mr. Mayes, that the world doesn't know about, that have been done in secret, which separates you from God?"

"Stop it! I don't need your accusations!" Derrick glared at the nun who was standing in the living room. An overwhelming dryness coated his mouth. "You don't know what I've been through."

"Have you seen the eyes? Fiery, iridescent, unnatural. They force you to stare back and reveal the darkest sins you've committed."

"Stooooop!" he yelled. "What are you doing to me? How do you know these things?"

Tears of shame formed in Derrick's eyes. All the thoughts of the things he had been doing; the drinking, the porn, even the suicidal notions were finally coming to a crescendo. He felt failure, a deep, disheartened sadness that was being enhanced by the fear of this new reality that was getting harder and harder to deny. His head hung low as he leaned against the counter. The nun walked from the living room toward Derrick.

"I've heard the whispers too. I've seen the eyes. Whether you want to accept it or not, demons are real." Her voice was low, gruff. There was a hint of controlled anger, not directed toward Derrick though. Sister Christina stood in front of him and removed the patch from her eye to reveal a horrid, hypertrophic scar that extended above and below a hollow eye socket. It was visible where two very sharp objects were inserted around the eye and viciously tore it out. The socket looked the same way Detective Mitchell described the way Dr. Leverty's heart was torn out. Derrick cringed at the sight of the mangled opening but noticed how her nostrils flared and her one good eye squinted slightly with the anticipation of her next thought. "You have to help me see Lucas. If the demon is there, I will attempt to banish it."

Derrick shook his head. "Banish it? Are you talking about an exorcism?"

Sister Christina repositioned the patch on her face to cover the old wound. "By implication only. A demon cannot be killed for it is not of this world. However, the demon can be banished. It's more like spiritual warfare. If the demon is present, it must be bound before it's banished."

"I don't fully understand. I mean, this still sounds very hokey, like some Southern Baptist nonsense meets some weird Catholic stuff."

"I didn't expect that you would understand. Most of what is taught in churches on Sunday morning simply leaves the warfare to that of angels and God. That thought process has never fully protected mankind. Christ brought us the Lord's Prayer which provides us peace of mind that our Father in heaven is always with us. Yet, it has never prevented us from being influenced by evil entities. It was merely the starting point to commune with the Father. Most other prayers, though claim to be the divine influence of God, were created by humans. Not saying that they are bad prayers, they simply offer meditation and serenity of the mind. There,

Mr. Mayes, I have considered your beloved psychology. In terms of exorcism, the actual Roman Ritual is merely a set of prayers and hand gestures, capable of casting out the demon, but it doesn't bind them. These prayers merely force the demon out of one person so it can move on to another."

"But if this demon you speak of is in Lucas and you said that you've been in its *deathly wake* since your first contact, by implication the 'binding' prayers you're referring to have not worked."

Sister Christina moved back into the living room and grabbed another photo. She handed it to Derrick who had followed her. "I have always been involved after the fact, too late to be effective. The closest I came was with a young girl. She had been raped repeatedly by an older friend of her cousin. The cousin lived in the household with her, and the older friend would make frequent visits. As it turned out one day, she entered the hospital in a catatonic state. The friend of the cousin was also rushed to the hospital that day with his genitals removed and forcefully jammed halfway down his esophagus. Cause of death was asphyxiation due to large obstruction."

Derrick winced at the mention of how the young man died. It certainly matched the grisly signature of the other murders. "How was this time any different than what you're seeing now?" Caution filled his voice.

"The demon hadn't completed its work. When I heard about the death of this nineteen-year-old boy, I went to see the girl in the hospital to investigate the scenario further. Since I wasn't allowed to see her in the hospital room because of police involvement and because I wasn't an immediate family member, I had to sneak into her room for the initial visit. No one suspected her of being the murderer. She didn't have an ounce of blood on her. Initial diagnosis was catatonia brought on by trauma, PTSD. Most believed she witnessed the murder. Upon arrival, I found her to be very alert, but very impassive. At first glance, she appeared to be recovering from the catatonic state, but I was keen enough to notice the young girl was having a profound effect on me. Pain ripped through my eye socket even though the nerves have been deadened for years. It was my sin that was coming out again. I knew immediately that she was under the influence of this demon."

"What happened?" Derrick asked shocked that this story resembled the way Lucas was acting that very morning.

"As the girl progressed and showed tremendous improvement, she was released from the hospital. I followed her home. The friend wasn't the only victim. Apparently, the cousin was the main perpetrator. He would allow his friends to partake in the abuse along with him. A day after she was released from the hospital, the cousin was supposed to be watching over her while members of the family were at work. That's when the attack came, being that I had followed the family as I did you, I heard the screams from the young man as the demon proceeded to torture him. *It* removed his eyes and had broken his back before I was able to come into the home. Once inside, the young girl was not herself anymore. Her face was contorted with rage and her eyes had a wicked glow to them." Derrick flinched as the picture of Hannah, contorted in anger with demonic eyes, flashed back into his consciousness. "I tried my best to stop it, to bind it, but I couldn't do it by myself. I was too weak, and the banishment quickly became a struggle for my own survival. The demon had me pinned to the ground, yet I was able to free my arm and roll the creature since it was only a young child's body. I was so enthralled with survival I hadn't realized that the creature abandoned the young girl and the thing I thought I was trying to strangle was gone. She died from strangulation. I was fortunate that I was able to call for help. The cousin survived. It was easy for the authorities to pin her death on him after he confessed to repeatedly raping her. He's currently serving two life sentences."

"So, you weren't able to save the *innocent* girl who had been repeatedly raped, possibly gang raped, in fact, she died by your hands, but you were able to save the rapist? Are you fucking kidding me?" Derrick spat. Anger bubbled from deep within. He turned from the nun and paced before facing her again. "You see, your perspective of things is lunacy, it's fucked up! Why? I mean, if these individuals were dogs, we would have euthanized them a long time ago. Why save them? Why was he allowed to live and not the girl?"

"The young girl's death was an accident, but a soul is a soul, Mr. Mayes. He confessed his sins. Every soul deserves a chance at redemption. Shall I judge you for your sins? Christ came to us for redemption and that is what the young man received. But consider his punishment versus hers. She's in no more pain and within the loving arms of our Savior. Whereas he sits, physically handicapped, blind, tormented by the knowledge of demons, and filled to the brim with regret. He's in his own personal hell. How long should he suffer for his sins? Are you capable of dealing out this judgment? The real thought is, who really was saved that day?"

"Whatever, it's still a matter of perspective. It's still fucked up!" Derrick put his hand over his face and sighed. None of this made sense, but simultaneously was the only explanation that connected all of the dots. He paused for several moments before asking, "So, when you *bind* a demon, what does that mean?" He breathed heavily with shock at even asking such a thing. Strangely though, the more he discussed the possibility of this being true, the more his own situation made sense. Derrick's disbelief began to collapse, and the dark reality of the unknown brought an unwelcomed chill. What he had been doing wasn't that far off from what he had learned about Lucas's parents. Some may even consider it on the same level of sinfulness.

Sister Christina motioned for Derrick to observe some of the other contents from inside her satchel. A small glass bottle of water, which Derrick could only assume was holy water, was capped, and tilted on its side. Two parchment-looking papers were tucked beneath what looked like other files. They were handwritten. Sister Christina handed one to Derrick. It read:

Binding

In the name of the Lord Jesus Christ of Nazareth, I stand with the power of the Lord God Almighty to bind Satan and all his evil spirits, demonic forces, satanic powers, principalities, along with all kings and princes of terrors, from the air, water, fire, ground, netherworld, and the evil forces of nature.

I take authority over all demonic assignments and functions of destruction sent against me and this servant of God, and I expose all demonic forces as weakened, defeated enemies of Jesus Christ. I stand with the power of the Lord God Almighty to bind all enemies of Christ present together, all demonic entities under their one and highest authority, and I command these spirits into the abyss to never again return.

I arise today with the power of the Lord God Almighty to call forth the heavenly host, the holy angels of God, to surround and protect, and cleanse with God's holy light all areas vacated by the forces of evil. This I pray in the name of our Lord Jesus Christ.

He finished reading the hand-written prayer and looked at the old nun. "I don't know. I mean everything you are saying makes sense considering recent events. But forgive me, this still seems like it came out of the medieval hysteria when people were burning heretics at the stake."

"Mr. Mayes…" She handed him the second hand-written prayer. "…this goes back much further than that."

Against Evil

Spirit of our God, Father, Son and Holy Spirit, Most Holy Trinity, descend upon me. Please purify this servant of God, mold them, fill them with yourself, and use them. Banish all the forces of evil from them; destroy them, vanquish them so that Your servant can be healthy and do good deeds.

Banish from them all spells, witchcraft, black magic, demonic assignments, malefice, maledictions, and the evil eye; diabolic infestations, possessions; all that is evil and sinful; jealousy, treachery, envy; all physical, psychological, moral, spiritual, and diabolical ailments; as well as any other spirits of death and darkness.

I command and bid all the powers who molest me—by the power of God Almighty, in the name of Jesus Christ our Savior—to leave your servant forever, and to be consigned into the everlasting lake of fire, that they may never again touch Your servant or any other creature in the entire world. Amen.

"How are these prayers any different than the other prayers?" Derrick asked as he passed the hand-written parchment back to the nun.

"It's not so much that they are different. More so the order in which they are read as well as this." She held out a pendant, an amulet that dangled from a black leather chord. Markings lined the edges of the round metal object. The inner circle was divided into four quadrants, again with strange markings and symbols that appeared to be astrological.

"What's that?"

"This is the seal of King Solomon. A seal against evil."

"Solomon? As the king whom God Himself granted wisdom?"

"Yes. This amulet in combination with the prayers will bind the demon so it can be banished."

"I don't know. This–this doesn't sound like *church* stuff anymore. It sounds more paganism, something the Catholic Church renounced many years ago."

"King Solomon was also very revered throughout Christian theology and through God's gift of wisdom, he had developed amulets such as this. Commercialism has diluted most of the trinkets that are sold online. Their true purposes have been lost within the silly naturalist's view of things." Her distaste for the association of Solomon and paganism was obvious in her voice. "Solomon was and still is the only person apart from Christ *himself* that was able to bind a demon. Now…this amulet in combination with the *Christian* prayers will banish the demon we seek from ever returning."

Derrick took the amulet from Sister Christina. It looked and felt old. It was heavier than he expected as if the pendant itself carried a heavy burden. "Okay, let's say, hypothetically that you're right. This–this demon entity is inside of Lucas. Then what?"

"He'll need to be restrained while I bind the demon. As before, I won't be able to do it alone. It's too strong and more people will be killed if we fail."

Derrick paused, taking a moment to ruminate over the strangeness of the nun's words. He handed the amulet back to her and shook his head. "These people…that you want to save…" He sighed again. "…never mind. I'm at odds with my own thinking and I can't believe I'm going to agree to this, but I'll take you to see him. We have to wait a little bit first. We'll go early this evening. That'll let some of the chaos at the hospital die down."

"I'm afraid we can't wait until later. We have to go back to the hospital now."

"No, that you cannot force me to do. When I last left him, there was a uniformed officer by his door and several others posted at the end of every major hallway. Neither one of us need to be detained. I said we'll go later and that's final. Lucas isn't going to be released from the hospital any time soon. They have not been able to get ahold of the only family member he has, and I have to sign off on any transfers to another facility."

"Lives, souls are at stake!" Sister Christina exclaimed as she paced around the living room.

"Right," Derrick said incredulously. "I could get fired for this, but in all my years as a case worker and even as a therapist, I haven't run across anything like this before. If you're right, then truly we have a larger problem on our hands. Given the strangeness of the events, I want to be prepared. So, while we are waiting, you're going to tell me everything again."

9

Sister Christina spent the next several hours explaining to Derrick all of the details involved with what she intended to do if she was correct about Lucas: how she needed to sprinkle the holy water on Lucas's head and body after she placed the amulet around his neck and then again after the first prayer to set the bind on the demon, and how the second prayer may need to be repeated several times to cast out the demon once it was bound and what to do if they drew too much attention.

Together they reviewed the case files she had, the newspaper clippings, the murder photos, and the possibility that things in the unknown were real. The time was now 6:35 p.m. In the cold darkness of an early winter's night, neither of them said a word as they drove to Children's Hospital in Derrick's Jeep.

Construction on Interstate 71 South toward downtown slowed them a bit, but everything appeared normal. Lights from the Rookwood Plaza shown bright against the dark sky as they drove past. Various other buildings and homes along the highway added to the glow. Yet, inside the Jeep was a dim, uncomfortable tension between Derrick and Sister Christina. On one side of the car was a cautious skeptic that challenged every thought, feeling, and experience thus far, but who had begun to realize that it had been a losing battle. Next to him in the passenger seat was a battle-scarred, unapologetic nun who was extremely rigid in her resolve. There was no talking her down from what she believed, no way to shed light onto a different perspective. Her doggedness was rooted in a deep spiritual belief that Derrick had often seen in some of the most psychotic patients of his. If she were to change her beliefs, something very profound had to happen, possibly even traumatic. Derrick hoped that it wouldn't come to this. He hoped that she was wrong, and that Lucas had improved to a level that confirmed this to Sister Christina. But this hope was a mere thread compared to the agonizing tangles of new questions that knotted his mind, repudiating everything he had held true over the years, all of his education and even his thoughts about the church.

Traffic continued toward downtown as Derrick took the Taft Rd. exit. The tiara atop *The Great American* building could still be seen through the leafless trees as he rounded the bend. Beautiful, it stood out against the cloud-covered sky. Yet, as pretty as it was, the city had a sinister backdrop now. A new reality had formed, but it was still cloaked in mystery and the unknown. Derrick glanced out the window at several young people walking to and fro bundled against the bitter cold. He assumed they were part of the University of Cincinnati that was just a few blocks away from Burnet Avenue. They looked young, still innocent, and full of life and dreams. They were unmarked by the ways of the world, the dark paths that could lead to pain and suffering.

Derrick and Sister Christina pulled into the parking lot of Children's. Derrick's stomach began to cramp, and a breathy gust of air passed by his ear as he got out of the Jeep. He looked all around in dismay as he held his stomach.

"It knows we're here," Sister Christina said as she emerged from the other side of the Jeep. She rubbed the area just below her eye patch as if nerves had suddenly come alive with a twinge of pain. The nun stared at Derrick.

"I should've brought my gun."

"It would've done you no good. This creature is about torment. The gun would've been used as a lasting torment for *you*, but not to kill." She paused to let her words sink in. "We have to hurry."

Derrick could feel the sting of the cold on his cheeks as he nodded in agreement to Sister Christina. As before, she appeared to be immune to the icy air. They were fortunate the police presence had been drastically reduced since the morning. There were a few uniformed officers standing in the lobby area, but there was no sign of Detective Mitchell or anyone else that was directly working the murder cases. Dorothy wasn't behind the information desk either, to Derrick's relief. Her shifts extended through Saturday but had obviously ended before they arrived. Though pleasant to talk to this was an odd visit that was time sensitive, and he didn't want to give off the impression that he was rushing. It needed to appear as routine as possible. No one would say too much to Derrick considering he often worked on Saturdays, but given the tragedies that struck the hospital, any odd behavior would stick out. This was a point that Sister Christina had trouble coming to terms with. Her mind was more one-sided.

Derrick and Sister Christina agreed to walk into the hospital separately. Sister Christina entered first and made her way to the elevator. Derrick followed, carrying her satchel of materials. To not look suspicious, Derrick waited for the next elevator. Inside, he could feel his stomach tightening. It was just as the nun had spoken about. He was not overly nauseous, but the cramping was definitely getting stronger. As the doors of the elevator opened, he stepped inside and quickly hit the close door button. Derrick did not want anyone else riding on the elevator with him in case the stomach ailment continued to grow, and he immediately got sick. With each floor that he passed, the pain in his stomach grew stronger. Stabbing, pulsing with pain that stirred up the acid forcing him to burp. It was the same as before. *Son of a bitch, she was right*, Derrick thought. *Every time I've come close to this kid, I've gotten sick.*

The doors to the elevator opened to an eerie setting. Derrick could see down the hall and though a few nurses were working on the mobile stations, only one nurse was at the main station. She seemed too preoccupied with her computer screen to even notice Derrick. Sister Christina was nowhere to be seen and the uniformed officer that was stationed outside of Lucas's room from earlier was gone. The feeling in Derrick's stomach gripped him tightly. Nausea intensified and he had to fight back the urge to be sick by taking several deep breaths. Something was wrong again. He quickened his step toward Lucas's room, but time slowed and sound was absent. The door was slightly closed so that no one could see into the room. Gently, Derrick nudged it open.

On the floor, he could see croc-covered feet sticking out from behind the hospital bed. Derrick's focus returned with a sharp breath that escaped his lips. A muted sound of choking forced Derrick to rush further into the room. Sister Christina was kneeling next to Corey Coleman on the floor. She was trying to get him to sit up but having tremendous trouble because of his size and her frailty. "What the fuck?" Derrick blurted out. Corey's eyes had been torn from the sockets. Blood poured from his mouth. As he gasped for breaths, Derrick could see that Corey no longer had his tongue either. Between his legs was a larger pool of blood. A gaping, torn hole in his scrubs revealed that his genitals had been torn off. All that remained were the fleshy parts from where it once was attached. Lucas was nowhere in the room.

"Towels quickly!" Sister Christina stated as she started to pull the sheets from the hospital bed to hold against Corey's wounds.

Derrick pressed the emergency button on the wall to alert help as he made his way into the bathroom. He opened the door to find the uniformed officer crumpled on the floor with his neck broken, head turned at a complete one hundred and eighty degrees. "HOLY SHIT!" Derrick shouted as he recoiled. The contents of

Derrick's stomach came rushing up as he turned away from the bathroom.

"I NEED THOSE TOWELS NOW!" Sister Christina shouted from across the room.

Derrick swallowed hard and reached over the dead police officer to grab as many towels as he could hold. He rushed back to where Sister Christina was trying to help Corey. Without saying anything, she grabbed a couple of towels from Derrick and shoved them between Corey's legs to slow the bleeding. Another towel she wrapped around his head across his eyes to help stop the bleeding there too. Blood continued to gush from his mouth. Corey's body began to convulse. Several nurses rushed into the room and immediately began to assist Sister Christina in aiding Corey.

Sweat dripped down the side of Derrick's face. Adrenaline caused his hands to shake. Each breath was intense, labored and he felt the room starting to spin. Derrick, in shock, slowly backed himself against the wall across from the hospital bed. More hospital personnel rushed into the room to assist Corey. Nurses and doctors all appeared to move in slow motion and the rapid heartbeat from inside Derrick echoed in his ears. *"Derrick...Derrick, I'm still here...we're still here...come to us...follow us...we're over here..."* The whispers blended in with Derrick's wildly beating heart but urged him to move from the room. All other sounds became muted, hushed as if Derrick were wearing earplugs.

He was mildly aware of Sister Christina calling out his name as he slowly walked into the hallway. Nurses, and doctors, rushed past him despite his dazed persona. Derrick felt drugged, drunk perhaps. His eyes scanned the hallway searching for something, anything to fixate on to stop the spinning. *"Heeeeere…this way…follow me…we're here…"* the whispers continued to urge Derrick away from Lucas's room. His head still scanning, searching for the source of the whispers, just as it was earlier with the picture of Hannah.

At the far end of the hall, unnoticed by everyone rushing, standing still, staring directly at Derrick, was Lucas. It was as though no one could see him except Derrick. Voices were still muffled; his stomach was still churning with acid and cramping. On the floor, there were droplets of blood that trailed down the hall. The closer Derrick got to where Lucas was standing, the more the piercing cramping pain in his stomach increased. It was horrible, as though someone had jammed a knife into his belly and was turning it in a circle. He couldn't hold back the feeling any longer. He stopped along the wall and got sick again into a small recycling bin full of paper.

Amongst the chaos, a nurse stopped. "Sir, are you alright?" she asked.

Derrick was breathing heavy. He nodded. "I'll be fine."

The nurse nodded too as Derrick pointed down the hallway toward Lucas's room. When he looked the opposite direction, Lucas was gone. Derrick forced himself to stand straight. The droplets of blood continued down the hall and through the exit into the stairwell. Derrick followed them. His dizziness had started to subside as he glanced around the vacant stairwell searching for the droplets. They went up, so did Derrick.

As he rounded the next platform, standing one level above him staring down the dimly lit stairs, was Lucas. Cockroaches poured over the edge of the steps and bedbugs crawled along the walls. They swarmed towards Derrick. Lucas's eyes burned bright, beyond the iridescent ruddiness Derrick had seen in the photo. His face was different, contorted with the same lustful anger, but it was paired this time with an eager expectancy. In a guttural voice, not entirely male, nor could it be identified completely as female, the demon hissed, "Sooo glad you followed ussss."

10

Lucas's face, arms, and hospital gown were splattered with blood. In his right hand was a fleshy piece of a body, Derrick could only guess belonged to Corey Coleman. "Who are you? Why are you here?" Derrick asked as he continued to fight back another urge to be sick. Bugs were now crawling over his shoes and clambering up his pant legs.

"We have many namessss, but *it* is the best for now." The voice of the thing echoed in the stairwell, overlapping and ethereal the same as the whispers. "As for why I'm here." The creature raised its hand that held the fleshy part of Corey. The blood on its arms began to dissolve into his skin as did the body part it held, until no signs of either could be seen anywhere on Lucas's body or in his hand. "They called me here."

Derrick moved upward a few steps. Cockroaches crunched under his boots, but he remained fixated on Lucas. "What are you?"

"Careful, the steps you walk here and in life are sssslippery. Keep drinking, Derrick. You're giving me sooooo much to work with!" Derrick paused on the steps and swatted away several bugs that had reached his waistline. He took notice that the thing redirected his question, exactly how Sister Christina had stated it would. His stomach was cramping, churning, and twisting, so much so that he had to lean against the railing because of the pain. Bedbugs immediately leapt from the railing onto his hand. Bite after bite forced Derrick to recoil. The mere presence of the demon was putrid, unclean, and unbearable. "How does it feel to have your stomach burning from the inside out?"

He threw up again in the middle of the stairwell. Roaches swarmed the vomit. The demon laughed, baleful and deep. Derrick spit to the floor and looked up again in irritation. "Why children? Why torment them? They're innocent!"

Without warning, Derrick was knocked to the landing. Before he had time to react, the creature was on top of him face-to-face. A tremendous pressure held him down. It opened its mouth to let biting centipedes rush forth. Derrick tried to move his head to avoid the insects, but they clung to his cheeks and bit at his neck. "Yesss, innocent, free of sssssin…blamelessssss, perfect and disgusting! I mock God's faultless gift to the world! They can't be harmed, only used!" The eyes were black with a fiery center that shifted between the color of flame and blood. "…he'll remember nothing, feel nothing, and will remain innocent and unscathed." The demon flicked its forked tongue, lizard-like across Derrick's chin releasing a foul breath of air. "…Until he chooses to follow your path Derrick, which leads to me! Come on…Pull that trigger, Derrick! End your pain! I'll be happy to retrieve you! Aaaaahahaha!" The laugh of the beast, echoed like the voice, overlapping. The pressure lifted.

Struggling to right himself, Derrick managed to get to his knees, wipe the repulsive saliva from his chin and look toward the upper platform just in time to see the door to the next floor click shut. All the bugs were instantly gone, and the malevolent laugh faded with the closing door. All disbelief dissipated inside Derrick. Shock and a new awareness of the unknown filled him. "God, what have I been doing? Please–please forgive me!" he whispered in the shadowy corridor of the stairwell.

Derrick reached into the satchel, removed the small bottle of holy water and the amulet of King Solomon. He wrapped the leather cord around the palm of his left hand and held the holy water in his right before rushing up the stairs through the door. It opened into a vast atrium, pillared, with glass skylights that shown out to the dark winter's night. The nighttime lighting was activated and cast a glow among the fake plants strategically placed for decoration. Derrick's head was on a swivel searching for the demon. He felt his stomach churning again. With a sudden force, Derrick was knocked from his feet to the floor again. Blood trickled from his mouth and dripped from his chin. The same sinister laugh echoed around him and into the high ceiling of the atrium. From his knees, Derrick yelled, "Where are you?"

"*Over here…right here…I'm heeeeeerre!*" The whispers passed over him in a ghostly breath. "Do you sssssseek to banish me, Derrick?" The demon stepped out from behind one of the large pillars.

Breathing heavy, Derrick stared at the unnatural movements of the creature as it shifted animal-like on all fours in a sideways direction. "You kill!" Derrick accused.

"Yes…I do Derrick…But try to banish me and it will *kill* the child."

"You lie!"

"Do I?" the voice was even more guttural than before. "Do it Derrick! I'll allow you…what will the world see? I'll force you to defend yourself, but the cameras will only see a child trying to defend himself against an overpowering man. They're looking for someone to blame." The demon shifted its voice to sound like Detective Mitchell, *"This was done by someone very sadistic and strong… But this also suggests that the person may also be stalking Lucas in some strange manner."* It laughed again. "It's remarkable what humansss choose to fit into their perceptionsss of reality. They'll pin all the murders on you…and what will they find on your computer Derrick…loads of porn…the worse kind involving God's perfect children being sssodomized…it'll add to the repulsive reputation you'll gain. You'll have no sympathy from your peersss. Let me go, *sssin* opened the door for me and I have entered."

"What about redemption? Mercy? You stole it from those people!" Derrick forced himself to stand. The pain in his stomach intensified. He spat blood to the floor from the gash on his lower lip.

"Aaaaahahaha!" The demon's laugh was deep and sinister again, resounding high into the ceiling above. "What about free will? Choice? The *invisible society* you called them, *leeches* you thought of them. God's fucking rejects chose their pathways. Their seemingly good intentionsss count for nothing! I feed on the sinsss they do in secret, isolated, only the vilest. I feed on the souls of the onesss that believe themselves to be invincible!" The demon hissed and flicked its tongue.

"Lucas's parents...they weren't invincible, why them?"

"Merely a starting point. I needed the child. Yet, innocent they were not!" Lucas's head bobbed back and forth under the demon's influence with eager, heavy breaths, anticipating Derrick's reaction. On all fours, it unnaturally remained, slowly moving closer to Derrick. He still clutched the bottle of holy water with one hand and his stomach with the other. "Their moment of weakness, alcohol...poor Lucas caught the wrath that night, concussion, never taken to the hospital, neglected and forgotten. It only happened once, but it was in their embarrassment, their fear of being accused that gave me what I needed. They verbally abused him, made him feel it was hisss fault. They threatened him that if he told anyone, the punishment would be worssse! Ssso, when it was time..." Lucas's body seemed to shift and grow in excitement. For a moment, it lifted back to a standing position with his arms splayed to either side, head bobbing like a snake. "...the blow they gave to him, I gave it back to them! I gave them what they only threatened to do him!"

The demon fell forward, back to all fours, forcing Derrick to defensively recoil. It flicked its tongue again. "Accidents happen! Wounds can heal! There are good people in this world…that do good things!"

"You're not referring to the sssneaky fuck, Dr. Leverty…" The demon let out another breath as it extended its tongue in excitement, still advancing on Derrick. "…the drug dealer. Oh yes, that nasty, heartless cusss was writing false prescriptions for amphetamine and methylphenidates to be sold on the streets, in schools…he has destroyed more families than he has helped…caused more heart attacks in young people, even deathsss…so I attacked his heart, and I shall feed on his sssinful soul!"

Bile in Derrick's stomach finally gave way and raced up his esophagus forcing him to double over in painful heaves. Seizing the opportunity, the demon lunged. Derrick uncapped the holy water and swiped his arm in the direction of the demon. Droplets of water splashed upon its face. "Filthy water!" the demon shrieked as it tumbled to one side. It leapt backward against one of the pillars and spider walked up the square column. "You stink of that whore of a nun! Did she tell you how we met? Why I came to sssee her?"

"It doesn't matter!" Derrick retorted still holding the bottle of water in one hand and the amulet in the other.

"Oh, it does Derrick! You're helping someone who witnessed and covered up multiple child molestations and rapes by a priest! She turned a blind eye to it, while child after child was abused. The priest would fuck them in the ass despite the desperate pleading for help and criesss of pain. He would then threaten them with damnation if they told. Oh yesss! He was a true man of *my* Lord and belonged down here with ussss!" the demon hissed in anger. Derrick stepped back from the demon that was still moving up and around the column like a spider. He felt a twinge of irritation at this thought. The demon could sense it on him. It laughed again, low and sinister, echoing around Derrick as if there was more than one creature. "Sister *Cunt* Christina lied to protect her church, even scolded a child that tried to seek her for help. When I came to claim the priest, I made sure that the fucking cunt *kept* her blind eye!"

"No…these are lies. You're–just trying to attack me. You know my thoughts about the church and you're using them against me!" Derrick reached into the satchel again and pulled the binding prayer from within. He glanced down at the paper and began to read the prayer aloud. A screech erupted from the demon's mouth, high-pitched and piercing. Buzzing horseflies also swarmed out and encircled Derrick. It forced him to drop the bottle of holy water as well as the paper, coercing him to his knees swatting at the flies. The creature continued the deafening shriek as it spidered its way down the column. As it hit the ground, it ran on all fours like a lizard, flicking its forked tongue at Derrick, compelling him to scamper backward until he felt his shoulders press against one of the potted decorative plants. The demon climbed Derrick's body until they were face-to-face again.

The pressure was once more too great for Derrick to move. Flies continued to buzz around his face. He held his left hand up just over his forehead to protect his eyes. The amulet still dangled from the leather chord that was wrapped around his palm. The demon stopped its advance. Its forked tongue licked at Derrick's chin tasting the blood that had dripped down. It breathed heavy and foul. "I know how you really feel, Derrick. You said it yourself to the bitch of a nun…" The demon's voice changed to Derrick's *"If these people were dogs, we would have euthanized them a long time ago."* It smiled a toothy grin at Derrick as it started to back away from him. "That trinket does you no good. You need *me* in this world. These people aren't fit to live, not worthy of the gift of life. You know it, Derrick, deep down…you know…"

Through heavy breaths, "Why don't you just kill me like the others?"

Its eyes slanted, and an evil smirk spread across its mouth. "I'm not going to kill you…yet. Though you have sinned, your sins have harmed only yourself. Not nearly as tas-ty! Not like that fat nurse, who was taking photos of children naked in their hospital gowns with his cell phone and ssselling them online, after he jerked off his own cock."

"But he was still alive! You only maimed him!" Derrick protested.

"When I'm ready to claim him, I will. Until that day, he shall see nothing, taste nothing, suffer greatly, with only the sound of my whispers in his ears. There will be no confession from him." The demon began to back away from Derrick.

"The cop?"

"His death was for interfering, quick, painless, a lost soul to me. But there are plenty others to feed upon, I don't need his."

"Why are you leaving me alive?"

"I'm not done with you yet. You're not ssstrong enough on your own! Knowing I'm real will torment your weak mind! In time, we will meet again."

Struggling back to his knees, Derrick watched the demon child slowly back away from him into the shadows. Only the iridescence of his eyes could be seen among the darkness. He reached for the binding prayer and holy water keeping his gaze locked with the demon's. "I can't let you leave," Derrick said as Sister Christina's words about the creature thriving on torment reverberated in his mind.

"Yes, you can Derrick, and you will. I can see into your heart. You want those vile fucks dead as much as I want to feed on them. Search within, remember all the cases you've had, the children you've treated because of people like the ones I kill. Remember the brooding hatred you have towards them and your job. They are mine now Derrick."

Derrick's words were frozen in his throat. His mouth was coated in dryness. Weakness overcame him from the bouts of being sick. The words of the demon child rattled around inside his head forming truths. He had great trouble accepting the fact that these people existed and operated in secret, in domains he could not reach to offer support. Yet, this thing could, but would not harm the child. Derrick sighed and dropped his head. At the same moment, laughter broke out within the atrium and echoed all around him. It began to fade as quickly as it came along with the horseflies. The eyes of the demon were no longer visible, and Lucas's body was nowhere to be seen. Panic ripped through Derrick. *No…No, I can't let you leave!* he thought. *Where are you?*

The sound of the automatic doors opening grabbed Derrick's attention. Without hesitation, he ran toward the noise. The churning, stabbing feeling inside his stomach was gone. Emptiness was all that remained. Beyond the automatic doors was a long corridor that led to the top level of the parking garage. Adrenaline surged inside Derrick as he raced down the glass enclosure and through the doors to the open parking space above the garage. Immediately, the wind bit at his cheeks and stung his skin, much colder than when he first entered the hospital. Lying on the frozen concrete along the center wall was Lucas, in nothing but his hospital gown.

Looking around to see if there was any sign of the demon, Derrick rushed over to where Lucas was lying. There was no one to help and Lucas's body was reacting to the vicious cold. It felt as if no heat was left inside the poor child and his skin was starting to dry out. Frostbite was not far behind. A strange sensation spoke to his cognizance. *The thing is gone.* Quickly, Derrick removed his coat and wrapped it around Lucas's small body. He placed the amulet over the head of the boy in the hopes that the demon would not be able to re-enter his body. Lucas was unconscious and completely unaware of what was happening, even as Derrick carried him back into the hospital.

11

Derrick sat on the edge of a hospital bed in the emergency room. A doctor looked over all his vitals and examined the gash on his lip. "You need some stitches. It looks like your teeth caused most of the damage. Almost went all the way through. Keep this on it while I get the stitch kit."

He nodded and placed the small cold pack against his swollen lip. Just outside the curtain area, Derrick could hear several people talking all around. The voices were indistinct and seemed to overlap with each other. Thoughts of the demon immediately filled Derrick's mind. He glanced down at Sister Christina's satchel that rested next to the chair across his bed. Tightness formed in his chest. His breathing became acute and fast. Just as Derrick had decided to slide from the bedside to grab the content from inside the satchel a voice rang through the crowd that Derrick recognized quickly. Detective Mitchell was talking with the hospital personnel. A moment passed, and a long breath of relief escaped Derrick's mouth as she entered his treatment area. Troubled, weary-looking, she sighed, "You alright?" Her voice was softer than before, more compassionate.

She was dressed formally as always, with her woolen coat draped over one arm.

He breathed in through his nose and released it slowly, "Few stitches, I'll be fine. You startled me."

"Sorry." Detective Mitchell sauntered further into the treatment space and sat on the edge of the bed with Derrick, placing her coat on the uncomfortable looking chair across from them.

"How's Lucas?" Derrick asked.

"He's awake and no frostbite, thanks to you…and he's talking."

"Really?" Derrick inquired more out of curiosity for what Lucas was saying rather than the fact that he was talking. Deep down Derrick knew Lucas was going to talk again. He knew that things were going to be okay with him.

"He's not say'n much. Doesn't remember a thing…at least not about the murder of his parents or the murders here at the hospital…nothing. Doctors think it's a part of PTSD and that his memory of these events may come out later with intensive psychotherapy."

"How's Mr. Coleman…Corey?" Derrick's voice was muffled from the cold pack, but Detective Mitchell still understood.

"They rushed him into surgery, but the prognosis doesn't look good. He lost a lot of blood and sustained some serious injuries. I don't understand how somebody could do that to another person." Detective Mitchell shook her head in disgust. "Beside the point, what brought you back to the hospital? What happened up there Derrick? Cameras didn't really reveal much."

Derrick removed the cold pack from his mouth so he could speak clearly. "When I went home earlier, I took a long nap. I felt better. Stomach had calmed down. I thought about what you had said and, well, I didn't want to hinder your investigation, so I planned to question Lucas a little more with a fresher mind." Derrick lied. Detective Mitchell eyed him pensively, expecting him to say more. There was no way he could tell the detective everything that happened, Sister Christina's involvement, what Lucas truly was. None of it could be proven. Worse, he knew what killed Lucas's parents, Dr. Leverty, and injured Corey. He wouldn't be able to talk about any of it, but part of him didn't want to. The people that were killed or maimed had caused so much pain and suffering for others that Derrick was having trouble rationalizing the dark feelings he now had. They had brought about their own destruction, yet the very thought of the demon, knowing it was real, unnerved Derrick and was bound to cause anxiety for the rest of his life.

"Go on…what happened when you got here?"

Derrick hadn't realized that he had stopped talking and was staring at the wall in front of him. "Right…when I got onto the floor, I was expecting to see the uniformed officer. When he wasn't there, I knocked on the door to Lucas's room and found Sis-ter Christina, is it?" Derrick played dumb.

"Yes, that's her name."

"I found Sister Christina tending to Corey in his injured state and Lucas was gone. She told me to get some towels from the bathroom and that's when I found the officer, dead. I suspect he too fought with the perpetrator, may have disrupted the torturous acts he was committing toward Corey. May have saved his life. I don't know, really." Derrick felt better about saying this. Though it was only a partial truth, but to paint him in a heroic light was going to be better for his memory, for his family, and for the police department. "Given that my stomach had been in rough shape from earlier, I got sick in the room when I saw his dead body. I moved into the hallway as more hospital personnel rushed into Lucas's room. The shock of the ordeal caused me to get sick again. That's when I noticed the droplets of blood on the floor and followed them into the stairwell. They led up to the atrium, where the perpetrator attacked me too. He hit me as I emerged from the stairwell." Derrick gestured toward his split lip. "I fell to the ground, dazed. I caught a glimpse of him running away from me, holding something in his arms. I assumed it was Lucas. When I heard the automatic doors open that led to the corridor, I forced myself to stand and ran after him. As I came out of the corridor, onto the parking deck, I saw Lucas laying on the concrete unconscious. The guy was nowhere to be seen." Derrick continued his lie.

"Are you sure it was a male?"

"Sorry, I just assumed, I guess."

"Did you get a good look at him? Were you able to see his face?"

"No, the lighting in the atrium was too dim and he hit me so quick, I didn't have a chance to see him." He hoped that the detective would believe his story. But really, what choice did she have except to believe him? Everything Derrick mentioned checked out, but the alternative was lunacy in the eyes of the police, it was the unknown, it was the unaccepted, it was the lies of truth hidden beneath a veil of perception.

Detective Mitchell crossed her arms and sighed again. She remained silent as Derrick repositioned the cold pack onto his lip. He had the feeling that Detective Mitchell didn't have any other questions to ask, that perhaps her case had grown instantly cold. "Well Derrick, there's a lot that needs to be done. I suspect that you'll continue to work with Lucas?" she asked as she grabbed her coat from the chair. Derrick nodded yes. "This goes without saying, but if you or he remember anything else, please give me a call."

"Will do," Derrick said, nodding his head slightly. The demon was right, knowing it was real and not being able to say anything, do anything, and not being able to help despite having full knowledge of who committed the murders, was torturous. He watched as Detective Mitchell slid the curtain back and proceeded to leave. *Why did the demon leave me alive? What did it mean by it wasn't done with me yet?* These questions among many others saturated Derrick's thoughts and cluttered his ability to think clearly. Random thoughts about Hannah, his mother, and even his job intermixed with the demon's comments. *Though you have sinned, your sins have harmed only yourself.* Guilt ran wide through

Derrick. He let his head fall into his hand as his elbow rested upon his knee. So many people tried to help him, but he turned away in a self-indulgent fit of depression.

Voices continued outside of Derrick's treatment area, all indistinct. He heard the curtain slide open again. Half-expecting to see the doctor with the stitch kit, he was mildly taken aback when a rougher, more weathered, Sister Christina stood in front of him instead. Disgust produced an abhorrent opinion of the nun. Derrick had worked tirelessly with children who were sexually abused to no real avail, and she had the power to stop someone from doing it but chose to protect her church instead of fighting for the weak. Derrick knew what she was going to ask, what she wanted to know. "It's gone…from Lucas," Derrick said before she had the chance to ask.

"Somehow, Mr. Mayes, I don't think it was that easy," she replied, doubtfully.

"Well, the particulars of it don't really matter do they?" He looked at the nun with different eyes, more outrage toward what she allowed to happen. *You deserve your blind eye sister*, Derrick thought, but didn't voice it.

"In fact, they do…did you complete the ritual the way I instructed?"

"It's gone." There was finality in Derrick's voice. Sister Christina clenched her jaw in disapproval. It was knowledge he had, but she didn't know he had, and it stirred inside him resentment toward her. There had been too many cases where children were abused in the ways she helped hide that didn't end happily. Many continued to have problems into adulthood and several of them became offenders themselves. In a few tragic instances, the children took their own lives to free themselves from the pain they had experienced. Given that Detective Mitchell stated Lucas was doing better, seemingly unscathed, and was starting to talk, he didn't feel the need to discuss the details of what happened. Lucas's case would simply fall back into the routines which were part of his job description.

"What did it say to you, Mr. Mayes? We agreed that-" Sister Christina started to say, but trailed off.

The doctor reentered the treatment space and slid a rolling tray over to Derrick's bedside. Atop the rolling tray was the stitch kit. "Okay Mr. Mayes, let's get that gash taken care of. Go ahead and lay on the bed."

"My satchel Mr. Mayes?"

Derrick motioned with his head to the location of the bag next to the chair.

"The pendant?" she asked as she grabbed the satchel and shifted some of the items around inside.

"The boy," Derrick curtly said. "Have a good evening sister." The tone in his voice was hardened, callous much like Sister Christina's, only it carried an implication of a newly attained knowledge of the situation, an implication that their dealings were complete.

"Mr. Mayes..." she tried to say.

Derrick swung his feet to the end of the bed and leaned back as the doctor instructed, ignoring the nun's attempt at the continuance of discourse. Sister Christina didn't acknowledge Derrick any further, but simply turned from the treatment area clutching her satchel, and walked away from him.

12

Three weeks had passed, and Derrick found himself at the entrance to his mother's church on May Street for Sunday morning service. It was very cold. Temperatures were still in the teens, but the sun was shining, and the skies were mostly blue except for a few rolling clouds. He assisted his mother through the front doors. Inside the atmosphere was warm and inviting. Members of the congregation moved about in all directions in preparation for the 10:15 a.m. service. Some were passing out brochures and others mingled, greeting those who came in the front door. "Ms. Mayes, so good to see you this morning! I hope God has blessed you in the past week," Pastor Marcus said as he greeted Derrick's mother.

"He has Pastor Marcus, He has. He brought my son Derrick back to the church."

Pastor Marcus turned to Derrick and offered a handshake. Derrick accepted it and grasped his hand firmly. "Praise God, I've been pray'n for you sir. I've been pray'n that the snares of the devil hadn't reached too far into your life and pulled you down a path of darkness. Praise God you're here now! Amen to that! Mmmmhmmm, amen!"

"Yeah, amen." Derrick felt his cell phone buzz in his pocket. "Would you excuse me for a moment?"

"Certainly, sir." Pastor Marcus turned back to Derrick's mother as he pulled his phone out to check his text message queue. From across the room, he could see Mary Ellen Ferguson. She was a stately woman, full-figured and homely looking. Derrick smirked as he looked upon her holding the hand of young Jeremiah, the child that she worked so hard to procure a foster placement within her home. Derrick knew she was more concerned about the money than anything, but she did provide a decent place for the children in their time of transition. Her home was clean, she would enroll them in school, and she would certainly feed and clothe them. Considering what Derrick had come to learn in recent days about other situations that children have been in, he finally expedited the paperwork for Jeremiah to be placed with her. Drawing his attention back to his phone, he had one message from Dr. Evans. It read:

How are you doing?

Dr. Evans was a good friend. Caring, heart in the right place and Derrick felt good any time he had the opportunity to engage with her. Derrick grinned at his phone as he proceeded to type his response.

Doing well. Haven't drank in 3 weeks. At church with mom.

I'm happy for you Derrick!

Even though JFS still had custody of Lucas, Derrick didn't need to spend as much time on the case. Lucas was talking now, and Dr. Evans was communicating any and all pertinent information to Detective Mitchell at the Cincinnati Police Department. Lucas's uncle had finally been reached and agreed to assume custody of Lucas upon being released from the residency home.

"Unbelievable," Derrick whispered. Everyone in the psychiatric field was going to tout this as a medical phenomenon and study the case files for years to come trying desperately to identify the reason behind Lucas's abrupt improvement. Derrick knew that they would be simply chasing their tails. He knew the real reason behind *everything* that happened to Lucas.

The music from inside the sanctuary began to filter its way into the lobby area where Derrick was standing. He smiled at his phone again before he slipped it back into his pocket. Assisting his mother, they walked down the blue-carpeted center aisle and sat close to the front, near the podium. Musty bibles and books of hymns lined the backs of the wooden pews. The sounds of the choir boisterously filled the open space. It was comfortable, pleasant. Derrick sang the hymns and listened closely, with keen ears to the sermon Pastor Marcus delivered. To no surprise of Derrick's, Pastor Marcus had turned the sermon into a bit of hell and damnation speech, but it was different this time. Hell was real. Forgiveness and mercy were a must. Derrick knew it, believed it, even if Pastor Marcus was only saying the damnation stuff to get a rise out of the crowd, to hear *Amen* being called out, to see a group of believers coming together as one. Perhaps it was the talent God had given to him. Perhaps it was simply meant to teach about the evil that existed in the world. Whatever the purpose, it gave Derrick a moment to think hard about the damnable things he had done and how even the smallest of sins could become a slippery slope toward darker things. Was that what happened to Sister Christina or any of the others affected by *it*? Derrick thought about Sister Christina's words, *A soul is a soul…are you prepared to issue out that kind of judgment?* "No," Derrick whispered only loud enough for him to hear.

Light from outside had shown bright through the tall windows. As the sermon ended, the light began to shift. Wind carried clouds across the sky and blotted out the brightness of the sunshine. Derrick could hear the wind whistling past the corners of the church, howling at times. The final hymn was sung, and the congregation bowed their heads in the closing prayer.

"Heavenly Father, In the name of the Lord Jesus Christ, be with us as we venture forth in Your holy and precious name. Be with us as we go forth in service of one another. Be our guiding light in a world so full of darkness. Protect us from the snares of the devil. Put your hands together and bless the Lord! Amen brothers and sisters Amen! Amen!"

With Pastor Marcus's final amen the congregation began to separate. Derrick's mother remained in prayer, so he sat next to her patiently waiting, taking in all the sights and sounds of the church. He hoped to find a little peace in his life, a few moments that he would claim to reflect on, to be still. His mother continued her prayer with a slight smile spread across her face as she whispered words to commune with God. Mary Ellen Ferguson's strident voice caught Derrick's attention. She was talking with a few members of the congregation and holding Jeremiah's hand, making introductions. Jeremiah seemed shy.

The light that was coming through the windows was drastically muted now. Wind blew hard against the building. The mere sound of it ran a chill down Derrick's spine, but a vague prickling on the nape of Derrick's neck unsettled him. A staleness had filled the air, replacing the dissipated incense. Derrick's mother continued to whisper her prayer, but with each passing moment, her words were getting louder as if someone was controlling the volume of her voice. The words began to reverberate around Derrick and blended in with the echoed beats of his heart. Pressure was building inside his chest, making it hard to breathe. A lump formed in his throat. Acid churned inside his stomach. Cramping coerced Derrick into rubbing his abdomen. Sweat formed across his brow and upper lip as the clammy feeling of nausea set in.

Mary Ellen Ferguson made her way down the center aisle to where Pastor Marcus was still greeting and talking with other members of the congregation. *This is just PTSD, anxiety…take some deep breaths*, Derrick reminded himself as he closed his eyes and took in air through his nose, releasing it slowly through his mouth counting backward from ten. His mother's whispered prayers grew louder and began to repeat. *"Our father who art in heaven, Our father who art in heaven, Our father who art in heaven, Our father who art in hell…"*

Derrick's eyes opened quickly. All around him felt dim and dark. No one else appeared to be affected the same as Derrick. His head moved on a swivel, searching for the element that was out of place. Everything felt wrong…again. The cramping in his stomach became so intense that it forced him to double over. His mother remained in her fixed prayer position, repeating the same line over and over again. *"Our father who art in hell, Our father who art in hell, Our father who art in hell…"* Acid bubbled inside as his stomach twisted in a stabbing pain. Unable to contain the vicious onslaught of painful heaves, Derrick threw up.

Cockroaches ran from underneath the pew in front of him and swarmed his vomit. *"Over here…we're here…I'm still right heeerre…"* The words were familiar, haunting. Panic raced through Derrick as he glanced upward, taking notice of Jeremiah who was still holding the hand of Mary Ellen. Jeremiah's head was turned entirely to one side staring directly at Derrick. His face was contorted into an eager, lustful, anger with eyes that were an iridescent ruddiness that flickered between the color of flame and the color of blood. *It* smirked at Derrick as the face of Jeremiah slowly reverted to normal and his head turned to face forward. Sound returned with vivid clarity. Others around Derrick, including his mother, had taken notice of his bout of sickness. Breathing heavily, he struggled to look around the horde of people trying to help. For a moment, he caught sight of Jeremiah standing before Pastor Marcus and heard Mary Ellen say, "Pastor Marcus, this is Jeremiah. He's going to be staying with me for a while. Please forgive him, he's a little shy. The child needs a good role model, though."

Pastor Marcus knelt, placing his hand on the shoulder of Jeremiah, beaming a great smile. "Amen little brother! What a pleasure it is! Ms. Ferguson, you can count on us spending some time together," he boldly stated glancing up at her and then back to Jeremiah. "You are welcome in this house!"

"No–not here, please God–no!" Derrick whimpered from across the room, but his words seemed to fall upon deaf ears. No one saw what he had seen, no one knew what he knew, and there was nothing he could do about *it*.

Acknowledgments

I would like to thank all those individuals who have encouraged me to continue with my writing pursuits. You know who you are, and I greatly appreciate you.

Special thanks to Randy Bell for helping me construct an authenticity to the characters in this story. Your input was extremely valuable and helped to make the unbelievable, believable.

Thank you to my Capstone Committee at Northern Kentucky University. Andrew Miller, Dr. John Alberti, and Kelly Moffett; all of you provided the best feedback and truly made this possible.

To my friend and artist, thank you Brendon Miller for sticking with this project and helping it to come to fruition with excellent artwork.

To the editing team at Reader2writer Press. Kayla Hardin and Bart Bishop, thank you both for your editorial skills and keen insights.

About the Author

After 16 years of experience (...and counting) teaching Middle School English and Language Arts in urban districts, two master's degrees, and a massive amount of black coffee, Brian came to realize the dire need for creativity and imagination in a classroom setting. Taught at The Ohio State University in his graduate program to design lessons and curriculum from scratch, yielded very minimal opportunities to indulge his profound love of writing. Ultimately this led him to Northern Kentucky University, where he acquired his second master's degree in English/Creative Writing. Since then, he has produced multiple lesson plans, materials, short stories for adolescents, and several other manuscripts for both adolescents and adults.